WANTON WAGER

Morgan Ashbury

MENAGE AMOUR

Siren Publishing, Inc.
www.SirenPublishing.com

A SIREN PUBLISHING BOOK
IMPRINT: Ménage Amour

WANTON WAGER
Copyright © 2009 by Morgan Ashbury

ISBN-10: 1-60601-479-X
ISBN-13: 978-1-60601-479-0

First Printing: June 2009

Cover design by Jinger Heaston
All cover art and logo copyright © 2009 by Siren Publishing, Inc.

Printed in the U.S.A.

PUBLISHER
Siren Publishing, Inc.
www.SirenPublishing.com

DEDICATION

To David. Thank you for your continued support of this dream of mine.

WANTON WAGER

MORGAN ASHBURY

Chapter 1

For one moment, Tabitha Lambert doubted her senses.

That hadn't been a near-miss on I-80 after all. I actually crashed, died, and now am being met by two of the most scrumptious archangels God has ever created.

She brought her car to a stop, turned off the ignition, and waited for the dust her tires had raised to settle. She regretted not putting the top up on her Porsche but it had been a beautiful day. Now the tawny clouds of dust caused her eyes to blink and tickled her nose. Focusing on the gorgeous vision of mankind before her, she used the fingers of her right hand to pinch her left arm.

Her senses screamed 'I'm alive' while her hormones chimed in, 'and raring to go'.

"Not dead. This is good. But maybe I'm addled." It seemed a reasonable explanation, since she was not only seeing double, she was instantly aroused.

The archangels appeared to be almost identical twins.

For a long moment she simply sat behind the wheel of her car, admiring the scenery. God knew this was the first vista she'd seen since moving west worthy of that endeavor.

The northern Nevada landscape sure as hell was different than her native upstate New York.

The archangels were tall, and seriously built. Tight worn jeans encased muscular hips and thighs. Shirts had obviously been discarded in the heat of the day, revealing masculine chests that glistened with sweat, and pecs and abs honed by the best gym in the world, hard physical work. She couldn't tell what color hair they wore as twin Stetsons covered their heads. The hat brims also hid a lot of their upper faces, but their mouths were visible. Their mouths looked sinfully delicious.

A woman would have one hell of a hard time choosing between these two hard-bodies. *What a rotten shame I've sworn off men.*

When those yummy mouths stretched into identical expressions of masculine smugness, Tabitha decided it was time to stop ogling and get to work. Uncle Sam wasn't paying her to lavish lascivious looks on local Lotharios. He was paying her to save wild horses.

Donning her poker face as a line of defense, she opened the car door and stepped foot on the Farenough Ranch—strange name for a ranch in her opinion—owned by the Kellers of Humboldt County, Nevada.

The file Tabitha's boss had handed her detailed some of the history of this sesquicentennial ranch—including the fact that the current owners were brothers, great-grandsons of the founder. It *hadn't* mentioned they were twin T-bone steaks waiting for some woman to gobble them up, blood rare.

I did not *just think that.* Tabitha took a deep, calming breath and approached the twin beefcakes.

"Can we help you, darlin'?" the man on the right asked.

He'd spread his legs just a tad, hooked his thumbs in the waist band of his jeans on either side of his belt buckle. It took no effort on Tabitha's part to envision those hands moving for that hunk of steel, opening it, and following through with an eye-popping zipper pull.

Tabitha Louise Lambert, get you mind off your glands! She reached down for her slipping professional demeanor with both hands. It was buried under about two feet of freshly fallen lust, but she found it, dusted it off, and fit it back into place.

"I certainly hope so. I believe my boss called ahead on my behalf. I'm Ms. Lambert from the Bureau of Land Management."

"Pleased to meet you, Ms. Lambert. I'm Jonathan Keller, and this is my brother James. And no, your eyes aren't deceiving you, we *are* identical twins."

His smile bloomed so easily Tabitha thought he must be used to the exercise. Now that she was this close, she could see wisps of dark, dark hair under those Stetsons. Two sets of eyes the color of the deep Atlantic sparkled with humor and male appreciation. Tabitha gave herself a mental kick to stop gawking and begin acting like the professional woman she knew herself to be.

"How do you do?" *There, that's better, very professional.* Aware of the correct protocol of the situation, Tabitha extended her hand, initiating the customary gesture of greeting.

Her palm met Jonathan Keller's and her sexual organs vibrated in response. She felt like a slot machine that had hit the jackpot. Any minute now her lights were going to flash and her bells start ringing.

She nodded as she broke contact, and had no choice but to repeat the gesture, extending her hand toward James.

Holy hell. They didn't look completely identical in appearance to her, but their ability to spin her reels was absolutely the same.

"A lot better than we were before you got here, darlin'," James said.

Tabitha blinked. Then she realized that he had taken her question as other than rhetorical and answered her.

"I'm here to talk about wild horses."

"Now that is a co-incidence, since it feels like a wild horse is galloping in my heart." Jonathan's smoothly delivered line, corny as it was, shouldn't have had the power to speed up her own cardio rate.

"Speaking of wild horses, that's a very nice car you're driving, darlin', considering that you represent my tax dollars at work."

James's teasing had nearly as lethal an effect on her as his brothers'. The pair of them were stirring her juices and lighting her fires.

Tabitha didn't want her juices stirred or her fires lit. She wanted to do her job and go home. Well, not home, exactly, because in her mind home was still Washington, D.C. But since divorcing Edward Lambert three months before she'd considered it plain good sense to get the heck out of Dodge.

Simply thinking about her ex put her in a nervous frame of mind. She didn't want to be nervous, either. Instinct took over, pulling out the old responses, the ones sure to make Ego-Ed's eyes glaze over.

"That's not just a car. It's a Porsche Boxster, S series, with a six cylinder Boxster engine, three point four liter displacement, three hundred and ten horsepower at seventy-two hundred rpm."

Two pairs of eyes didn't glaze over. They lit up.

"Oh yeah? What's the acceleration rate?" Jonathan asked, as he and his brother both passed her and went to look at her fire engine red baby.

"Zero to one hundred in five point three seconds."

"Sweet." They said in unison.

She had to give them both credit. They didn't exactly salivate, nor did they touch the car. They looked, and looked well.

"Holy cow, it's got PDK! How do you like that?" James exclaimed, looking as if he really did want to touch.

Apparently he knew cars. Not many Americans were familiar with the new Porsche Dopplekupplung transmission. A button on the steering wheel replaced the familiar gear shift and clutch.

"Now that I'm used to it, I love it."

"So you're really into cars, darlin'?" Jonathan asked.

Oh, he'd better not say 'darlin' to her in just that tone too often, or she would be nothing more than a puddle at their feet. Tabitha closed her eyes and called on every bit of will she possessed.

She pulled her thoughts back to the conversation and tried to filter out the physical effect these two were having on her. Never in her entire life to date had she become so aroused simply by talking, and talking about cars, at that! "Not especially. Why would you ask that?"

The brothers shot each other a look she couldn't interpret. The expression on their faces when they turned their attention on her again wasn't hard to read. Her libido began to chant a 'let's go' litany when she realized they were as attracted to her as she was to them. It was time to gain control of this situation.

"Gentlemen, please." She thought she put the same inflection into her voice as her former middle school principal, Wicked Witch Westerly.

"Well, our mother wanted us to be gentlemen, but I'm afraid there are times when we're anything but." James's confession seemed heart-felt.

"In fact, there are times when we can be downright wild and wanton." Jonathan's tone was no less repentant. Both brothers were mocked by the twinkle in their eyes and the sexy smiles kissing their lips.

Tabitha couldn't hold back her laughter. They might be dangerous men to be around, but they had certainly lifted her spirits when she hadn't known that's exactly what she needed.

"I really did come here today to discuss business. And not monkey business, either."

"Well, Ms. Lambert, now that you've given us the gift of your laughter, why don't you come on inside? Mary, our housekeeper, has made fresh lemonade. We can sit down and talk about the wild horse program. But you have to tell us your first name, and use ours in return. We're not so formal in these parts."

Tabitha thought quickly. The presence of a housekeeper sounded good, as did the lemonade. And since the brothers Keller had been a huge help in the BLM's wild horse program in the past and were about to be again, she supposed that she, on behalf of a grateful government, could tolerate a bit of teasing.

"All right, Mr. Keller." When his right eyebrow went up, she nodded. "James, then. And my name is Tabitha."

Both men stared at her, eyes wide. She had no idea what she'd done to elicit that reaction. She tilted her head slightly to the left and asked, "What?"

"You got my name right."

His bewildered tone just confused her more. "James isn't a difficult name to remember," she said lightly.

"It's not, no. But James and I were doing our best to distract you after we introduced ourselves," Jonathan said.

As she focused on him his face colored slightly.

"And while we were distracting you, we changed positions." James finished for his brother.

"Kind of like a human version of three card Monte, only with just the two of you?" Tabitha felt another laugh coming on.

"Never thought of it in those terms, but yeah," Jonathan said, then sent another look to his brother that she couldn't interpret.

"Do that with everyone you meet for the first time, do you?" She guessed the twitch at the corner of her mouth that she couldn't control told them she wasn't upset.

"Habit of a lifetime," James agreed.

"Kind of hard to break," Jonathan chimed in.

"I'm surprised it works. I mean, you look a lot alike, but I can tell the difference between you. It's not hard."

"Not even our mother can tell us apart!" Jonathan protested.

"Well I can." Then she smiled. Since they were being so friendly she decided to satisfy her curiosity.

"Why Farenough?"

"Not 'fair nuff,'" James corrected. "'Far enough.'"

"And that would be on account of Gertrude Schultz Keller, our great grandmother," Jonathan added.

"Legend has it that Great-Grandpa was searching and searching for just the right place to put down roots," James picked the narrative back up. "The evening they ended their travels for the day here, Gertrude refused to go one mile more. Said she'd gone far enough."

Tabitha laughed. That made twice in the same half hour. The bad thing about that was the Kellers might consider her the flighty sort. The good news was that for the most part, the impact of their sex appeal had ebbed just a little. Feeling as if she really had the upper hand for the first time since she arrived, she turned and headed toward the large ranch house. Then she looked over her shoulder and gave them her best smile. "Just for the record, that three-card Monte thing? I've never been taken. Gambling is nothing more than a matter of statistics and probabilities. My daddy taught me that. He's the one who gave me the Porsche, by the way. Your tax dollars had nothing to do with it. It was a reward."

"I'm probably going to regret it, but I have to ask. Reward for what?"

She'd heard the shuffling of feet behind her and knew they'd changed their positions again. Stopping when she got to the porch, she waited until one of them stepped past her and opened the door.

James opened the door but it was Jonathan who had asked that question. So she turned, gave him a bright smile, and said, "Why, Jonathan, for divorcing my husband, of course."

* * * *

Jonathan stood next to his brother, both of them silent as they watched the dust swirl behind Tabitha Lambert's Porsche Boxster S series as it wended its way back to the county road.

He turned to look at his brother.

"Did you feel that?"

"I sure as hell did. And do you know what? Sweet and sexy Tabitha felt it, too."

"Yeah, she certainly did."

James planted a hip on the porch railing and turned to look at him straight on. "You know, we really should have seen this coming, all things considered."

"You have a point. Hell, we've shared just about everything else all our lives. Why not fall for the same woman at the same time?"

"Mary-Lou Benton and Katie Franks," James said.

"Our senior year in high school. Mary-Lou was the first girl I was ever half-way serious about—just as Katie was yours." He had an idea he knew where James was headed with this conversation. "Pamela Crawford and Amy Jenkins," he returned.

"Second year of college," James confirmed. Then, more seriously, he said "Ginger Henderson and Rachel Martin."

"Yeah, they were the two that finally did it for us, weren't they? I remember you saying, after we broke up with that pair, that it was a damn shame we couldn't just marry the same woman." Jonathan *had* known where James was going with this. They generally could finish each other's sentences and thoughts, as a rule.

"Well, I only said that because not once in all our dating history have our steadies ever gotten along, *or* been tolerant of our close relationship."

Jonathan scowled. "Ginger tried to convince me that you'd threatened her." Even nearly two years later, it rankled. "No, you're right, none of the women we've ever dated have really *gotten* us, or our bond. Period."

"No, they haven't. But I think Tabitha might," James mused. "And that's not just my glands talking. Though she certainly got them working again after what feels like a drought of massive proportions."

James turned his head, looking in the direction Tabitha had gone.

"That's the kind of woman who makes me think we should reconsider our pact," he said.

"Yup," Jonathan agreed. "That woman would be worth giving up a no-relationship pact for. In fact, I think she'd make one man a fine wife."

"Brother, I'm thinking she'd make *two* men a fine wife."

Jonathan looked at his brother speculatively, and felt his smile grow at the same time he watched his brother's do the same.

"Agreed. Just how do we go about making that happen, exactly?"

James cocked his head to the side, a slight nod as if pointing after their recently departed guest. "Statistics and probabilities," he replied softly, "and some good old fashioned horse trading to set it in motion."

Jonathan felt his smile widen. "Brother, I like the way you think."

"That's because, brother, you think the same way I do."

"So I do, James, so I do."

Chapter 2

Sitting at a stranger's kitchen table and talking wild horses and burros while sipping lemonade created by epicure extraordinaire Mary did nothing to put an end to the hornies.

Neither had driving like a bat out of hell back to her office in Carson City, with opera music—which she loathed—blaring full blast on the car radio.

She'd sat through a department meeting with her boss, two agents from the Battle Mountain District Office, and a couple of outside consultants. The meeting, like all meetings, had dragged on way too long and covered way too little of real significance. And at the end of it she'd been just as hot, just as in need of an orgasm as she'd been since she'd met the Kellers several hours before.

Now her work day was done, and as she drove the twenty-odd miles to her home on the outskirts of Reno—she'd bought a house because she hated apartments—she knew it was time to take matters into her own hands.

Literally.

Of course, she'd rely on Sol, as she had been doing these last few weeks, to help her achieve maximum satisfaction of the orgasmic kind.

One good thing about having a Self Operated Lover as opposed to a husband, Tabitha thought as she shifted the Porsche into sixth gear, you didn't have to worry about finding him in bed with your best friend.

Before acquiring Sol, she'd spent her personal recreation time since her divorce and for several months before with Bob—her Battery Operated Boyfriend. But he'd shorted out when she'd taken him in the shower one evening, and that had been the end of that affair. The next day she'd bought Sol. He was definitely low tech, but built for pleasure, all nine and a half by two and a half, authentic-to-the-touch cyberskin-covered inches of him. He might not vibrate, but he was aces in the shower.

Sometimes a woman just needed it wet and wild and wanton.

Up until today, Tabitha would have sworn she'd been adjusting exceptionally well to the total devastation her personal world had suffered six months before. She'd come home one day, uncharacteristically taking a half day sick leave because of a cold, and walked in to see her husband fucking her now former best friend. She'd gotten an eyeful, then turned around and walked right back out again.

Now here she was a continent away from Ego Ed the ex, with a good job, a nice ranch style house with a small yard. She'd burned out Bob, picked up Sol, and had been certain her life lacked nothing.

Then she'd taken a drive to Humboldt County, met the brothers Keller, and had come away with an itch in serious need of scratching.

Activating her garage door opener as she approached her house, she counted the seconds until the thing was up. She parked her Porsche smoothly, got out of the car, and activated her anti-theft alarm.

The garage door closed, as did the door that led from garage to kitchen behind her as she nearly ran toward her bedroom.

Four minutes later, Sol in hand, she stepped under the hot pulsing spray of her shower.

Sol didn't seem to ever mind waiting beside the body wash on the chest-high wire rack in the shower stall until she was ready for him.

Steam and pulsating water began to dissolve tension, and Tabitha tilted her head back, closed her eyes and sighed. Drenching her blonde hair while the tiny fingers of water massaged her scalp, she thought showers were one of the most civilized—and decadent—inventions of all time.

Ranking right up there with Sol, of course.

Eyes firmly closed, she reached for her tube of body wash. As the light floral scent permeated the steam surrounding her and the soft, silky texture of the lotion caressed her skin, Tabitha released every care and real-world thought in her head.

Her hands, delicate in their touch, stroked over her plump breasts, fingers coming together to tweak and tug already erect nipples. The sensation of silkiness carried by rivulets of water cascading down the flesh of her front stoked her arousal.

Unbidden but inevitable, the vision of two men, womb-mates, materialized center stage in her imagination.

She considered herself a healthy woman with a healthy sex-drive. Of course she'd indulged in fantasies from time to time. What woman didn't at one point or another wonder what it might be like to have two lovers at the same time? What woman didn't dream of being pleasured by two sets of hands, two mouths, and two cocks?

Tabitha had before, of course. So she didn't chase the fantasy away. This was the first time ever her two love-masters had faces and names. The change tingled and aroused more hotly than a simple, generic, faceless mind-romp.

She moved her hands over her body, down her sides, across her belly, then up and over her breasts again, and imagined two sets of work roughened, masculine hands mapping her flesh. Then down, slowly, until fingers brushed through the wet blonde curls at the apex of her thighs.

Silky, teasing, there then gone, the touch of fingers gliding across her labia aroused and heated. Inner muscles clenched, as if to grab and gobble any flesh that neared, the urge to quench a voracious hunger surging through her with each heartbeat. Bolder now, she played her fingers down, full palm contacting an aching, arching clitoris.

"Mmm," the sound, forged in the very depths of her soul, rumbled up, unconscious and uncontrolled.

Her sex cried out for more substantial attention, as she imagined one man, strong, compelling, holding her firm as another knelt before her, his fingers urgent and strong as they worked inside of her, sliding in and out as a mouth, hot and moist and hungry, drank from her.

Water continued to cascade over her, hot, melting, as one hand continued to stroke swollen, heated flesh while the other reached for Sol.

She moved the toy across the front of her pussy, the head spreading open the quivering lips, as if it was a real cock seeking fire and silk.

"Ahh…" she sighed as slowly, inch by inch she worked Sol deep inside herself. Her inner muscles clenched the familiar, craved presence as her hips tilted forward. She raised her right leg, balanced it on the lip of the tub, and could almost feel the heat of a male body behind her, holding her firm for the thrusting of another in front.

Slow, steady, the rhythm built, the cadence ascended. Only one goal ruled, only one thing mattered. Stroke by heavy, gliding stroke, she reached for it.

"Take him well, darlin'. Take him well, and then you'll take me."

Imagination whispered, images pulsed and vibrated with life, until she could see them, hear them, smell them, *feel* them.

"You belong to us. Confess it."

Yes. The word ricocheted in her mind, a weapon, a prize. Harder, faster, deeper, the movements inside her became everything. Tabitha cried out, the climax crashing over her, exploding out from her pussy, shivering over her flesh to consume her entire body. Her clit trembled from the shocking, ecstatic jolt of the orgasm. Her wail keened as wave after wave of rapture flooded her body and soul, filling, cascading, claiming, consuming.

"Oh, God." Nerveless fingers dropped the dildo as aftershocks rippled her skin, tightened her womb and beaded her nipples.

Water, pulsing and cooler now, rained down upon her as she leaned against, clung to the shower wall. With hands not quite steady, she reached out, closed the tap.

For long minutes she rested there, the occasional shock wave wracking through her. She laughed, but the sound emerged weak, and maybe, she thought, just a little bit desperate.

That was probably the best orgasm she'd ever given herself. That was the good news. The bad news, she admitted to herself as she slid the curtain out of the way so she could step out of the tub, was that she was still horny.

No, it's more than that. Closing her eyes, Tabitha acknowledged the truth. She wasn't just horny, she *hungered*. She hungered for the feel of twin hands on her skin and hard, twin cocks inside her body.

And she had no idea what in hell she was going to do about it.

* * * *

Derek Hamilton entered the seedy bar, far from his usual type of haunt and far enough from his own back yard that no one would recognize him. He walked like a man with purpose, like a man unafraid to pound hell out of anyone who got in his way.

Both were more than impressions. He had not so much a purpose, as a mission. A deputy sheriff didn't make much money, and he'd grown up lower middle class. He'd lived his entire life so far on a pittance.

Today's meeting was about to change all that.

The man had chosen a booth in the back corner. Derek slid onto the seat facing him. Saying nothing, he reached into his inside jacket pocket, then tossed four photographs on the table.

"This should give your client an idea what's available," he said.

A waitress ventured over to get his drink order. One look had her scurrying away. Derek tried not to laugh. Everyone who knew him would swear he was mild mannered, even tempered, affable even. No one would ever believe he could look—or be—so hard, so cold.

Good-old-boy was the image he worked hard to project, for it was the image that served him best. But that wasn't him, not really, not by a long shot.

He'd grown up knowing that his family lived a blue-collar, scrape-for-a-dollar existence because they'd been cheated out of their birthright. And he didn't have to look far to see who had prospered because of it.

There were only four families in his part of Humboldt County that could trace their ancestry back to when the county had been created by the Utah Territorial Legislature in 1856. The Hamiltons—his family—was one. As were the Scotts, the Franks and those *bastard* Kellers.

The land the Kellers called their own should have been *his*, would have been his if history had been written just a shade differently. He'd searched through all the old family records, spending hours in his younger days with his paternal grandparents, looking for proof of what he'd long suspected. There was no proof, of course. Leastways, not anymore. But he *knew* the truth. And by God, so would everyone else one day.

Wilhelm Keller had cheated Derek's great-grandfather in the late eighteen hundreds. Orville Hamilton had been in business with Keller when both families had come to this part of the world. Three years later, Keller had bought out Orville's share for next to nothing.

That single act set the stage for the generations that followed. Anger began to bubble inside Derek as he thought about the unfairness of it all.

He'd always had to make do, always just surviving when others around him had everything handed to them on a silver platter. His father worked construction all his life, going from boom times to bust times. His mother was a teacher at the grade school. It had never bothered his folks to be blue collar workers living from paycheck to paycheck.

Shit, they had never cared that he was embarrassed by the house he lived in, the clothes he wore, and the trucks he drove. They never cared about him at all.

They didn't think it was any big deal that he'd had to stand back and watch those Keller boys—freakish twins that they were—have all the best of everything just for being *born* Kellers.

He'd done his best over the years to pretend to be their friend, and had swallowed his pride—and his bile—every time being close to them got him some crumbs off their table. It was his connection to them that had provided his summer work and his summer fun as a teen. He knew he'd worked harder than either James or Jonathan. He smiled now, thinking the things he'd learned those summers on the Farenough Ranch were sure going to come handy now.

He'd graduated high school, but there'd been no trust fund set up for *his* college education. His father had taught him construction, and he'd saved his pennies so he could take some courses in investigation and law enforcement. That had been a smooth move on his part, and allowed him to move out of working with his hands and with his old man.

The law didn't pay as well as construction, but it had other fringe benefits. Rotten Rosie, the local madam, kept him supplied in weekend playmates in exchange for his looking the other way as they went about her business. A few of his former classmates kept him supplied in booze and any electronic gadget he needed, like the digital camera he'd used to take the pictures his new business partner was looking at now.

Funny, he'd taken those courses so he'd learn how to uncover the facts of the past. But getting this job had introduced him to an entire new realm of possibilities. If a man was smart—and no one could deny that Derek Hamilton was a smart man—he recognized business opportunities when they came his way.

The man sitting across from him was one such contact, a man who had a network of friends and businesses overseas. Some of those friends would pay hefty dollars for the opportunity to own an American wild horse. He'd done his research too, and was keeping his eyes out for some of the rarer breeds. Spotting one of them would net him in the tens of thousands of dollars.

In the mean time, Bormann had mentioned that one of his contacts would pay top dollar for a particular kind of horse.

It would take him no time at all to rope such an animal. Half a day, tops.

"I'll scan these and send them to my client. But I am reasonably certain this is indeed what he wants. I should be able to get back to you shortly. Perhaps by e-mail."

The man Derek knew only as Bormann slipped the photos into his own pocket. Derek tore off a scrap from a napkin and wrote his e-mail address on it. Bormann pocketed that, as well.

"I have another client who is interested in establishing a...new trade route. I was wondering if you knew of an area, fairly remote, where planes could be brought in low to drop off supplies?"

He'd figured a couple thousand dollars for a half day's work capturing wild horses was just the beginning. And here now was the proof of that. Did he know of an area? He sure as hell did. The same area where the horses could be had, the same area that should have been his.

He paused, giving a look around to ensure no one could overhear.

"As a matter of fact, I have the perfect area in mind."

"I thought you might."

This was going to be bonus. Not only would he finally be hauling in the kind of money he deserved to make, but he'd be shoving it to those damned Kellers in the bargain.

He'd be smart, he decided impulsively. He'd establish his presence in the area. That way if he was seen, then his being there would be accepted as normal.

And he would arrange clues, evidence, for when this gig was up. Crime did pay, just not necessarily for the long haul. When he got wind that his time on this project was drawing to a close, he'd plant that evidence and those clues, and have investigators heading in one direction, and one direction only: the Farenough Ranch, and James and Jonathan Keller.

Chapter 3

"Well hello, Mr. Keller. Stella on the front desk told me you and your brother had arrived. If you'd let me know you were coming in, I'd have set up a private luncheon for us." James Keller turned at the sound of those purred words. The woman was a looker, no doubt about it. Tall, lushly curved, with flame red hair and siren-green eyes, Phyllis Demeter undoubtedly turned heads wherever she went, but it was her eye for detail and her head for business management that had won her the position of managing the second major holding in the Keller empire, the Aces and Jacks Casino and Hotel.

"Hi, Phyllis. Sorry I didn't let you know we were coming. It was a last minute kind of thing. You're looking well."

"Thank you. And you don't need to give me advance notice. I'm always available for you. It's been so long since we've spent any time together. Just let me clear my schedule, and I'm all yours for however long you need me." Her voice was smooth, the gentle caress of her hand on his arm the action of a friendly acquaintance, but James heard alarm bells going off in his head.

The casino had benefited from Phyllis's deft hand on the reins for the last two years. But now as he really looked at her, James began to wonder if the lovely Ms. Demeter wasn't hoping to be more than just an employee.

James knew he'd never given the woman any reason to think that he'd be interested in a personal relationship. He and Jonathan felt very strongly about not crossing certain lines. Messing with female employees was one of those lines.

He kept one eye on the front door—Ms. Tabitha Lambert would be walking through it at any moment—but he knew he had to diffuse this newly perceived development immediately. Sometimes ignorance really was bliss. He'd simply respond as if he hadn't just gotten a whiff of the woman's charged up hormones.

"There's no need to clear your schedule. You've done a good job of keeping us apprised of the day to day operations and implementing our operating procedures. No need to waste your lunch hour on us, either." He kept his tone polite, and scrupulously eliminated any hint of chumminess or familiarity.

He'd have to talk to Jonathan about this latest unwanted situation, but later. His eyes were drawn back to the front doors as a certain blonde came into view. Ms. Lambert had just walked in, looking adorably confused and delectably good enough to eat.

"You'll excuse me, Phyllis?" He mated the rhetorical question with a nod of his head—a purposefully dismissive nod—and turned, making a bee-line for Tabitha.

"This is a strange place to have a meeting, James," Tabitha greeted as he approached.

Damned if her ability to distinguish him from his brother didn't please him enormously. He hadn't missed that Phyllis had called him Mr. Keller, instead of by name. He and Jonathan insisted on being on a first name basis with most of their employees. Her formality had been a cover for ignorance—she hadn't been certain which one he was when she approached, since he'd not put on his name tag. He dropped his casino manager from his thoughts and focused on a much more pleasant subject.

"Tabitha, it's so good to see you again." Unable to resist, he took her hands, brought them to his lips, and felt the pulse in her wrist speed up when he kissed them.

"We only just met yesterday. You make it sound as if we've been apart for ages." She'd tugged her hands back, and James shot her what he knew was his best cheeky grin.

"Well, darlin', it feels like ages since I last looked at your luscious self."

"Are we waiting for Jonathan, then?" her voice had just a bit of frost to it.

James smiled. Her eyes were flashing daggers, but her cheeks had turned pink and her breathing had hitched. Damn, he really liked this woman.

"Jonathan is upstairs in our office checking in with the ranch manager. He'll join us in the board room shortly."

"Your office?"

"Yes. It's on the third floor. But we thought you'd prefer to meet in the board room. It has a neutral feel to it, and is on the main level. Fairly close to the gaming floor, but we'll close the door so we shouldn't be distracted by the sounds of gamblers."

"You…own this place?"

"We do. Now, that's a nice smile."

"It's the name of your casino. Reminded me of a card game my daddy and I used to play."

"Really? Well *our* daddy renamed it for my brother and I, when we were about ten. It's our nick names combined. Mine's Ace and my brother's was—is Jack."

"Ah, I see. Do they still call you that? Ace?"

James motioned for her to precede him as he guided her toward the edge of the gaming floor. The closer they came to it, the more they could hear the noise. Mid morning, about an hour from lunch, and the casino was full. Tourists made up most of the clientele. The professionals and the serious gamblers who either lived in the area or traveled a circuit would come in later in the evening, usually after ten.

"No," he answered her, turning to look at her full on. "Not since I gave up playing poker on a regular basis." Then he leaned closer. "Aces and Jacks, man with the axe, natural sevens take all."

"Yes!" Tabitha's face filled with delight, her eyes no longer holding that edge of chill. "I thought that was just a game Dad made up!"

"No, ma'am. Played it a time or two myself. Been thinking of playing again, though, just lately. Are you any good at it?"

"At…poker?"

Oh, they were on the same channel, no doubt about it. Those lovely light blue orbs wore a bit of a glaze, now, and her nipples had just betrayed her by poking straight up and pushing against her top.

"At whatever game is on the table." Hell, he was getting aroused just looking in her eyes. When they got her naked, it was going to be one damn fine good time. But fast. He had a feeling their first time was going to be very, very fast.

He waited for her response, and when it came, he gave her high marks for sheer daring.

"Why James," she purred as she leaned into him just a bit, "I can play any game you care to name. Play it, and win it."

"Darlin'." The sound of his brother's voice didn't break the mood. James hadn't noticed Jonathan's approach, but he stood behind Tabitha now, his body almost brushing hers. James smiled, because he could see the presence of another wasn't dampening Tabitha's fire, either. When Jonathan bent forward just a bit, when he ran a hand down her back, James wondered that there wasn't steam rising from all three of them.

"Those are the very words we were hoping to hear. Would you care to make a little wager?"

* * * *

Tabitha wasn't used to being on the receiving end of smart mouths and smart moves, but she had been getting a steady supply of both since meeting these two hunks, and that was going to have to change. She needed maneuvering time, so she'd excused herself just before their meeting got underway. Yes, she'd used the bathroom, but she'd also called her boss and arranged for a few days off.

Since the time was owed to her and had been offered just the week before, the man was happy to comply. Now if things went the way she thought they might, she would have the option of participating, or keeping to herself for a few days until the dust settled.

In the mean time she was horny as hell again. The board room, tastefully decorated and very professional looking, fairly sizzled with heat despite the cool reading on the thermostat.

More aroused now than during yesterday afternoon's assignation with Sol, she had to beat back the images that had been flooding her mind ever since Jonathan had come up behind her and run that big hot hand of his down her back.

Naked, writhing, one lover rising up over her while the other cradled her, lifting her leg, spreading her to receive him…

"Can we get you anything, Tabitha?"

The question from James's smug, masculine mouth pulled her out of her fantasy into the not-at-all erotic setting of the meeting.

"Get me anything?" She hated the squeak in her voice, and wondered if she could brazen it out through the rest of this meeting.

"You know…coffee….juice….water? Just tell us what you want, darlin', and we'll do our best to give it to you."

Oh, they were clever. They knew exactly what they were saying, and exactly what they were doing. And they knew the effect they were having on her, too.

If life was a poker game, now would be about the time to call their bluff. They were teases, the two of them. Tabitha looked down at the documents before her.

First she would take care of business, then she'd turn the tables. She'd bet once she did, one or both of these sinfully sexy men would turn tail and run.

"No, I'm good. Actually this meeting is the last thing on my agenda today. I have a few days coming to me, and I thought I'd take them. So let's finish this up—and let me say, on behalf of the United States government—thank you for your generous offer."

"Just giving back."

Tabitha found it interesting that Jonathan could toss out an outrageous sexual innuendo without batting an eyelash, but blushed when offered sincere thanks for what truly was a generous offer.

The use of Farenough land for a wild horse sanctuary, complete with donated feed and irrigated watering spots should the pastures suffer undue drought, all underwritten by the Kellers, would be an enormous help in the Bureau's wild horse and burro program.

All the existing holding facilities were in Kansas and Oklahoma. This one, in the west where so many of the horses and burros roamed, though not a holding facility, would provide an additional sanctuary that could be monitored and maintained—and all without taxpayer money.

All that was left to do was to turn the paper work over to the attorneys. Jonathan offered to have one of the casino staff courier them over to Tabitha's office. Looking from one to the other of the Keller men, Tabitha wondered if they both maybe had an idea that the little game they'd been playing since they'd met the day before was about to come to a turning point.

"Why, thank you. That means's my work day will be done all that much sooner. Then I can really begin to relax and…play."

A knock announced the arrival of a young woman, impeccably dressed in business casual. James scooped the file folders off the table and handed them to her. If the woman thought it odd she was being asked to take the files to the BLM office in Carson City, she didn't show it.

In moments Tabitha was alone once more with the brothers Keller, although the door to the meeting room remained open.

"Playing is highly underrated. So tell me, darlin'…what kind of game did you have in mind?" James's voice, smooth hot fudge over pure vanilla ice cream heated her blood and melted her joints.

"Have any idea where a girl can get a little private action? I was thinking maybe a few hands of Texas Hold 'em." It wasn't hard to make her voice breathless. She'd felt breathless since meeting the pair.

"Oh, we can arrange a private game, no problem," Jonathan said in a voice no less smoky than his brother's.

"We were thinking maybe one game. One hand. With a very personal wager." James smiled as he offered that.

"But what if I want to play more than just one hand?" Was that her, putting that cock-teasing pout into her voice, licking her lips just to incite these two sexy studs? *Was she out of her ever-loving mind?*

"Now, darlin', you have to know there's more than one way to play...and more than one game in town." Jonathan pitched his voice low, and Tabitha felt it rumble in her belly.

"What did you have in mind?" They were good, damn good. Tabitha felt the moisture gathering between her thighs and the humming low in her womb as if her inner atoms were busy cleaning house because they knew that company was coming. Thank goodness she was still sitting down. The men wouldn't know her knees had gone weak.

On the other hand, they were both standing, and it only took one glance to realize they were both already semi-hard, and that their relative positions put their cocks on nearly the same level as her mouth, making that water, too.

Tabitha felt totally aroused and completely reckless. *Not a good combination at all.*

"If one of us wins, you come home with us today. You become...ours. We'll pleasure you until you melt; both of us together, and one of us at a time. And we bet you, Tabitha Lambert, that together we'll be able to meet every one of your needs and fulfill every one of your fantasies. You'll become...addicted to us. And darlin', this game would be for keeps." Such emotion filled James's voice that Tabitha realized what was happening between them wasn't entirely a game. These men were serious—or at least believed themselves to be. She swallowed hard and looked from one to the other.

Even though she was well rid of her ex-husband, the failure of her marriage and the dissolution of the relationship had stung. Not playing now, she gave them her honest-to-the bone reaction. "What good would that do me? You'd be putting me into a position where I would have to choose between you. That's a recipe for heartbreak if ever I heard one."

"Oh, no, darlin'. You've missed the point entirely. We *do* want you to choose. But we want you to choose us both, not choose *between* us," Jonathan explained.

Oh my God. They were absolutely serious. They were offering her something she'd only admitted a hunger for in her own personal fantasies. Holy hell, this room had become awfully hot, awfully fast.

"Um…and what do I get if *I* win?"

"Anything you want," Jonathan replied for the both of them.

"And you expect me to accept this…this wanton wager?"

The men looked at each other, then looked at her. "We can smell your heat, and you're no coy miss. You're a woman with one hell of a good brain who knows her mind, and makes her own decisions. And you're a gambler." James smiled as he said all that, obviously enjoying the shock she knew she wore. She'd been married to Ed Lambert for over a year, and these two men already knew her better than he ever had.

"Come on, darlin'. Take a chance," James finished.

A shiver coursed down her spine. It wouldn't be the first time she'd done something totally impulsive. But it sure as hell would be the most interesting. And hell, when it came right down to it, either way the cards fell, how could she possibly lose? She was an unattached adult woman with a growing itch and time on her hands.

She answered them both, but directed her words to the one she sensed was in control. "All right, Ace. Cut the cards."

Chapter 4

Jonathan wasn't much of a card player. Usually. He and James enjoyed a division of responsibilities. He took the lead on the ranch while James was in charge at the casino. He supposed, really, that of the two of them and in most things, James had always been the leader, and he the follower.

That had never bothered him. What most people never got about them is that they weren't so much copies of each other as they were mirror images. James was more outgoing, easier with people, and smoother with the words. Jonathan was quieter by nature, but a bit more able to tune into other's emotions.

He and his twin made a damn good team, and Tabitha Lambert suited them both.

The sound of cards being shuffled called his attention back to the present. They were in one of the private card rooms located just off the main gaming floor. The table was kidney shaped, with a well for the dealer, a tray to hold plenty of chips, and room for seven players.

Whether by design or just fate, they sat with Tabitha between them. James would receive the first card, and he himself the last.

"Just player's chips," James said to the young man who stood as dealer. "We're not playing for money. And since we're only going to play one hand, we'll suspend the usual blind open and raise."

"Just one hand, Sir?" Curiosity lit the dealer's face, but he didn't press beyond the one question.

James shot him a huge smile. "Just the one, Billy." Trust James to know the young man's name. "And don't worry, you'll get the going rate."

Dealers pulled out of rotation on the floor to deal in the private rooms got a special tip. If he knew his brother, Billy was going to make out very well for the few minutes he'd be working in here.

"Thank you, Sir. Cut?" He offered the deck to James, but his brother passed the honor to Tabitha.

Tabitha placed the colored marker card about a third of the way into the deck. Billy then shuffled and dealt.

Jonathan waited until his brother and Tabitha looked at their cards first. Neither gave a clue as to what they'd been dealt. One day he would love to watch an honest-to-God poker game between his twin and the engaging Ms. Lambert. He'd bet they'd match each other, bluff for bluff.

Jonathan looked at the two cards he'd been dealt. A pair of sixes. Gold or garbage, James would say, depending upon the flop.

"I'll open. Ten." James set the chips in the center of the table.

"And five more." Tabitha's voice was cool.

"Hell, I didn't even do anything and already it's costing me more," Jonathan said that with a smile tugging at his mouth.

"Everything costs, Jonathan."

Tabitha's tone was kind, and when she looked at him, he gave her a wink. "True. But some things cost more than they should have had to, darlin'. That is going to change."

An expression of calculation replaced the complacency she'd worn. Good. He might not be as slick as Ace over there, but he was a force to be reckoned with.

He tossed his fifteen chips into the center. Jonathan added the five he'd been raised.

"The flop," Billy announced as he dealt three cards and turned them face up in the designated area on the table close to the chips.

The six of diamonds, Ace of diamonds, and ten of clubs stared back at him.

Most people couldn't read his brother at the poker table, but Jonathan wasn't most people. James was awfully pleased with the flop.

And Tabitha—unless he was mistaken—was not.

"Another ten."

"Call."

Jonathan nodded, and tossed his ten into the pot. Without seeming to, he watched Tabitha. She looked at her hole cards, then shot sideways glances to first James, and then him.

"The turn card," Billy announced as he dealt one more card face up. The Ace of clubs, which gave him a full house, sixes over Aces. James looked pretty pleased with the card, too.

"Fifty," he announced, moving that many chips into the pot.

Tabitha looked at him, then turned and looked at Jonathan.

She closed her eyes, then sighed. "The river card isn't going to change the outcome of this game. I fold." She tossed her two cards face down toward Billy.

Quick as a wink he scooped them. Jonathan nodded, then repeated Tabitha's move.

He had no problem letting his brother stand as the outright winner of this particular game.

James likewise gave his cards to the dealer, and got to his feet. He held Tabitha's chair, then looked at him. Jonathan caught his unspoken message and nodded.

"We'll help you get your things," James said quietly.

Jonathan smiled. The cards might be in the hands of the dealer, but the game was definitely on.

* * * *

Phyllis Demeter looked up from her conversation with one of the croupiers to watch as the Kellers escorted that blonde out of the private gaming room and across the lobby.

"Excuse me, Peter." She left her employee and followed after the small procession, planning to corner James once the tart—whoever she was—had left.

The appearance of the woman earlier had disturbed Phyllis. James—at least she was reasonably certain it had been James she'd been speaking to—had left her cold, practically in mid-sentence when she'd arrived. Then Phyllis discovered that after being holed up with her in one of the meeting rooms, both brothers had taken her into one of the private gaming rooms. She'd seen to it that Billy had covered the action there, and knew she'd get a report from him later.

But for now, she meant to pick up where she left off with James. He was wearing a tie, and the other one was not, so the man she'd been speaking to *had* to have been James.

Wish they'd both wear their damned name badges all the damn time. Then at least she could be certain which one was James and which Jonathan.

It was James she wanted, of course. James was the one with the smarts, as far as she could tell. He also seemed to enjoy the city more than his brother did. Oh, if she had a cowboy kind of fantasy she might think about giving Jonathan a ride. But he was a rancher, and Phyllis considered herself an avowed urbanite.

How those two brothers got along so well was totally beyond her.

Just as Phyllis crossed in front of the front desk, she realized the Kellers were leaving. As she watched, one of them stroked his hand down the blonde's back in what looked like an intimate gesture. The other took her hand and walked with her in one direction while the brother who had petted her went in another.

Well, what the hell?

"Ms. Demeter, may I help you?"

Phyllis turned and gave one of her best smiles to the young man assigned to the concierge desk. His name was Kevin, and he'd been with the casino only a few months. A recent college graduate, he was fresh faced and eager as a young puppy to please. And she'd bet he knew who was who and what was what. She'd noticed he paid attention to his surroundings.

"Good afternoon, Kevin. No, unfortunately, there's nothing you can do to help. I was hoping to catch Mr. Keller before he left. Nothing urgent. Unless…you don't happen to know who that young woman was with them? She looked awfully familiar, but I simply can't come up with a name. It must be middle age setting in."

"You're still young, Ms. Demeter. Actually, I believe the woman is an agent for the Bureau of Land Management. Earlier, Jasmine said she had to courier documents for her over to the BLM office in Carson City."

Ranch business. "That's it. Thank you, Kevin."

"Any time, Ms. Demeter."

Phyllis turned away, a sense of relief settling over her. Not personal, then. She dismissed the gestures she'd witnessed. She'd noticed in the past two years that the Kellers were both what she would call "touchy-feely" kind of men. Not with their staff, of course, but with friends and relatives.

That thought caused a frown to crease her brow. Maybe the blonde bimbo was more to one of them than just a professional contact. The relief that had so recently settled over her fizzled.

It would be wise, she mused, to find out just who that woman really was and what her connection was to the Kellers. Phyllis had a plan, and it was well past time for her to put that plan into action.

She made good money managing this casino. It was by far the largest establishment she'd run in her career to date. She did a hell of a good job too, if she did say so herself. But she wanted more out of life than to be a casino *manager*—an employee. She wanted to be the owner. And the best way to do that, she'd decided when she'd celebrated her thirty-fifth birthday two months ago, was to marry the boss.

She was an intelligent, confident woman. James Keller wasn't bad to look at. Neither, when it came right down to it, was she.

Phyllis knew how to use her femininity when she had to, and she'd never met a man who could resist her when she'd set her mind on having him.

She'd have James Keller well in hand before the year was out. So she'd make some phone calls and see what she could find out about that female who worked for the government.

One thing was certain: no blonde bimbo was going to mess things up for her.

* * * *

Tabitha pulled her car into the garage. The electric door slowly closed as she turned off the engine. Inside, she was shaking with need. She refused to think about what she had just done, what she had just agreed to do.

The man beside her reached over and stroked her arm. "We need to go in so you can let Jonathan in the front door."

"Yes." Her shaking intensified as she left the car and entered the house, James Keller close on her heels. Tabitha nearly smiled, thinking she was even hornier right at this moment than she'd been the day before on her mad rush to her assignation with Sol.

What she was about to do—willingly, even eagerly—was going to be a hell of a lot more satisfying than playing with her dildo in the shower.

As she opened the front door to admit the man who stood there waiting, one thought zipped across her mind. *My God, I haven't even kissed either one of them yet.*

Jonathan proved how tuned in to her he was at that moment. He stepped forward, dropped something he'd been carrying, and cupped her face in both his hands. "There you are, Tabby-cat."

His words brushed her lips just before his mouth settled on hers. *Oh my God.* His flavor flooded her senses, a tidal wave of ambrosia that snaked through her blood to the pit of her belly. Heat swamped her body as a million hormones were released to run amok through her system. Pleasure and arousal became one when Jonathan swirled his tongue against her lips, when she opened to him. Velvet strokes stoked the fire of her passion. Her tongue danced with his, as eager to drink him as he seemed to be to drink her. Tabitha's nipples hardened, and her panties caught the moisture dripping from her sex.

Her knees weakened, and she would have slumped to the floor if James hadn't pressed his body against her back just then. He slipped his arm around her waist, his hot palm open and pressed against her blouse.

The twin sources of heat sent a delicious vibration humming in her blood. Jonathan weaned his mouth from hers, and she whimpered at the loss.

Then strong male arms turned her around and a second set of masculine lips claimed hers. Spicy and rich, James's kiss tasted as potent as his brother's and proved just as flammable. Her arms wound around his neck as her mouth opened, eager to take his essence in. Hot and wet, James's tongue stroked and delved in a rhythm that was heavy, slow, and deep. Trusting the arms that came around her from behind, she let herself be supported by one man as she kissed another, surrounded by the heat of them both. Their scent went straight to her head, a primitive recognition that demanded she open herself completely to their possession.

Jonathan's left hand held her up while his right caressed her breasts through the fabric of her blouse.

"You're so hot for us Tabby-cat," James purred the same pet-name Jonathan had given her. He reached a hand down and pressed it against her clothing, right at the apex of her thighs.

Tabitha couldn't hold back her cry of need, she couldn't help but roll her hips forward, wanting more than that teasingly light touch.

"Did you bring the condoms out of the truck?" James asked of his brother.

"Got the box and our stuff right here, James."

Tabitha hadn't noticed that he'd brought a black travel bag in with him. But she'd heard a *thunk* just before his lips had taken hers. He must have dropped it as soon as he'd set foot in the door.

"We want to stay the night, darlin'. Our first night together, here where there'll be just the three of us. Hope you've got a good sized bed."

"This is moving so fast," she said, a moment's hesitation licking at her nerves.

"You can say no at any time, Tabitha. Bet or no bet, you know that, right?"

Damn them for putting the ball and the responsibility firmly in her hands. A part of her wanted them to just sweep her away. Wasn't that how she came to be exactly where she was standing?

But she was a woman who owned her decisions, always. She had no way of knowing how this was going to play out, or where she would be at the end of it all. But for now, her body craved both these virile men.

There was no reason not to take what was being offered. No. That sounded wimpy as hell. She would be honest with herself, and these men with whom, somehow, she had connected on a very basic level almost instantly.

"I don't want to say no. I've never taken two lovers at the same time—never thought I ever would, though I can't deny a fantasy or two. I don't want to say no," she repeated, making sure her gaze met each of theirs. "I want you both. I want you both every single way I can have you."

"Well then." Jonathan gave her a hug at the same time he bent down and nuzzled her ear. James reached forward and began to undo the buttons of her blouse.

"We've never shared a woman before, either. But it feels right. *You* feel right." James's words reverberated in the pit of her belly where they fluttered and aroused.

"Let's move our party to the bedroom," Jonathan suggested. He slid his arm from around her, allowing her the freedom to stand on her own two feet, and to lead.

"It's this way."

Chapter 5

Tabitha had closed her bedroom drapes this morning against the midday sun. The house came with central air, but she liked the additional implied coolness of the semi-darkened room. She heard their footsteps behind her and stopped when she reached the bed. Turning, she faced them. Enough light remained she could see both men were aroused. Twin cocks tented the front of well fitting pants.

Tabitha had never considered herself a voluptuary. She'd never been ashamed of her body, but neither had she enjoyed a lot of lovers. There had been a couple of men before her husband, and not a single one since. She'd never been an exhibitionist, either, and sex in the last year—before her divorce—had become pedantic and disappointing. In short, she'd considered herself at best mediocre in the bedroom.

Jonathan and James were looking at her as if she was the hottest sex goddess of all time.

She couldn't begin to describe the feelings coursing through her as she finished the job James had begun of opening her blouse. Slowly, she tugged the garment from the waistband of her skirt. Two pairs of eyes watched avidly as she let the blouse fall from her shoulders to the floor.

"Let me now, darlin'," James said. "After all, I started undressing you. And I always finish what I start."

One step, then another, and he stood before her, his gaze riveted on hers. The heat from his body, close yet not even touching, seared her. She drew in a shaky breath as he ran a feather-light touch down her chest. He dipped a finger under the edge of her bra, teasing her right nipple. The explosion of heat in her womb and a second release of moisture between her legs made her whimper.

"You're so sensitive to our touch. I watched you melt when Jonathan touched you, and now you're melting for me. What an incredible turn on."

She felt like she was two women. One stood transfixed, aroused, ready to combust as James reached behind her with one hand and flicked open the hooks on her bra. The other could see the effect watching her with his brother was having on Jonathan. Knowing that she had both these men in thrall made her feel her power as a woman in a way she never had before.

"Please," she couldn't take the craving and not having, not for one second more. Her bra hit the floor, and she reached for James's hands and gave him her breasts.

"Yes." She sighed her pleasure. *He has magic hands.* Just the caress of his fingers on her flesh had her close to rapture. She wanted more, wanted it all and growled in frustration when he teased and tantalized, when his fingers grazed, his hands cupped, then released.

"You need to learn some patience, Tabby-cat."

Tabitha had closed her eyes to better enjoy the sensations shivering through her. At the sound of Jonathan's voice, its nearness, she opened them to find him standing before her. James had moved a bit to her right to make room for his brother.

Jonathan reached behind her, his hand caressing her naked back and coming to rest at the edge of her skirt. One twist of his fingers and she felt the button on her skirt give way. Moments later the garment pooled on the floor around her ankles. Twin hisses told her the men liked her stockings and garters, and her very tiny thong.

Had she dressed this morning with them in mind? Not consciously. But after the inferno they'd inspired in her the day before, she wondered now if maybe she hadn't had a premonition that this moment would be in her future.

"Lie down on the bed, darlin', crossways. We're going to feast on you now."

Tabitha aimed for a controlled, graceful descent. But her eagerness over-rode her ego. She didn't care at that moment if these two studs thought she was a shameless hussy hungry for their hands, their mouths and their cocks. She was, come to that, and it felt wonderful. Sprawled on the bed, she spread her legs, sensing they wanted to be the ones to take the thong and stockings off her, and praying they'd be quick about it.

They were quick, but in stripping the clothes from their own bodies. They were also shedding their civilization at the same time, she sensed, and with a speed she could only describe as meteoric.

Two erect cocks sprang free of confinement, and Tabitha knew she was about to experience heaven.

James knelt on the bed to her right. Because he was the first to get closer, her gaze focused on him, on the sheer beauty of his body. His chest and arms exuded strength and virility, the dark hair that dusted his pecs and trailed down his abdomen to nestle his sex gleaming even in the low light. His cock stood erect and bounced with his movements and his response to being the subject of her adoring scrutiny.

"No second thoughts?" he asked as he moved closer, as he grasped his penis in a way that said he would feed it to her if she wanted it.

"None. James, *please*."

But he didn't do the expected, didn't deliver that hard part of himself for her oral pleasure. Instead, he stretched out beside her. Jonathan came down on her left, but her attention was captured by James. Stroking his hand through her hair, he turned her head so that she faced him and then settled his mouth on hers.

Subtly different, this kiss epitomized carnal pleasure. Slow, deep, his tongue explored, tasted, dominated, and she felt seduced. Hot, delicious and wet, his mouth fed her the potion of arousal, taking her higher, farther, than she'd ever been before. When he eased, when he weaned his lips from her, another hand gently guided her head to the left, and Jonathan was there to woo and entice.

Tabitha lost herself in the sheer pleasure, in the mind-numbing eroticism of their mouths on hers. *Only kisses* she thought when words would form in her sex-drugged brain. Only kisses and she was already on the verge of a climax. They kept taking turns, taking her higher.

Just when she thought she was going to come apart at the seams, they laid hands on her. Breasts and arms, belly and thighs, masculine hands stroked and petted, pinched and cupped. Unable to control herself, she writhed under their ministrations. Deep masculine chuckles teased but she didn't care. She would have rushed them, rushed this, but they had set the pace and thank God for it. They lavished her with attention, and taught her without words that she could take more than she believed she could, that she could soar higher than she'd thought possible. Her skin shivered, her nipples puckered, and the dampness from her sex nearly became a rain.

"Now, darlin'," James cooed as he plunged two fingers deep into her pussy.

"Oh, God!" Tabitha screamed as the orgasm exploded over her, bowed her off the bed, as the electric jolts cascaded from her clit to her fingers and toes. Wave upon wave of bliss consumed her, ravaged her.

Her lips had abandoned Jonathan's when she'd begun to come, but he had continued using his mouth on her, licking his way from her neck to her breast. Now he sucked her nipple into his mouth, using his teeth to nip and his tongue to soothe, and her orgasm only settled down a little. And then it began to build again.

"Your pussy squeezed my fingers so hard, Tabby-cat. Will you squeeze my cock the same way?"

"Oh God, I…I can't," she felt the arousal climb, knew she was going to come again. She honestly didn't think she had anything left, that she could bear another dose of such extreme pleasure. Shivering, shaking, she reached for the climax even as she wondered if she would survive another. Sound and movement penetrated dimly, the tear of plastic, jostling motion and the sound of a slick slide.

Jonathan released her nipple and eased away just as James came down over her, settling between her legs.

"Yes you can. Let me come inside you, Tabitha. Take my cock into your hot little pussy."

Had she believed she couldn't take any more? The moment she felt his latex-covered cock against her wet, sensitive folds, she burned to have him deep, deep inside her.

"Yes. Yes. Fuck me, James. Now, fuck me now!"

"*Tabitha.*"

She wrapped her arms and legs around him as he pushed into her. His cock felt bigger than what she'd been used to and she reveled in the sensation of being filled completely.

"God, woman, you feel so damn good around me. So hot."

He had sunk into her completely and for a long moment seemed content to just stay put. Tabitha surged her hips, so close to another orgasm she thought she might die if he didn't move.

"More. Damn it, James, fuck me!"

"Soft and slow? Or hard and fast? How do you want me to fuck you, darlin'?"

"Hard. Fast. Deep. Yes. *Yes.*" Reality became only this moment, only this man filling her, fucking her, so that the all she wanted in the whole world was to come and come and come. He gave her what she'd demanded, hard and fast and deep. The bed shook with the force of his thrusts. When he pushed his chest away from her, her arms slid to the surface of the bed. When he lifted her legs and spread them wider, when he placed one foot on the floor to brace himself so he could change his angle, she felt him hit deeper and harder.

A stroke on her hair had her turning her head. There, Jonathan knelt, his cock just inches from her mouth. Hungry, she opened wide, and when he slid his hand under her head and lifted her just that little bit, she closed her lips around his penis, eagerly sucking him in.

Jonathan's taste proved instantly addictive, and Tabitha marveled she'd lived all these years without him. James stretched her vaginal passage with the pounding of his cock, and she wondered that she could ever have believed herself incapable of giving and taking such pure pleasure.

"Oh sweetheart, you have a fabulous mouth." Jonathan's impassioned words fluttered her belly, and watching the pleasure take him filled her with pride. She swirled her tongue along his length then began a steady, rhythmic suction that tore a cry of surprised wonder from his throat.

"I'm close, baby. Will you come for us? I want to feel your pussy squeeze my cock when you come."

Tabitha had no control as her two lovers gave and took with equal abandon. She couldn't seize her rapture, she could only surrender completely, could only receive and give at the pace these two hot studs set.

Jonathan grunted, wrapped a hand in her hair and inhaled a deep breath through his teeth. She felt the quiver, the tell-tale twitch. Reaching her hand up, she cupped his balls and squeezed gently.

James licked two fingers and then laid them on her clit and rubbed fast and light.

She came hard, soaring instantly to the height of passion, her pussy convulsing, James's shout announcing his orgasm at the same time as her mouth milked Jonathan of his seed.

On and on the pleasure pulsed, the waves of rapture crashing over and through her until Tabitha felt completely spent.

"My God." Jonathan's fervent benediction was followed by his collapse on the bed beside her. James's body lost the battle with gravity and for a few short moments he sprawled on top of her, giving her all his weight.

Tabitha liked the feel of his body pressing her into the mattress every bit as much as she like the feel of Jonathan resting close beside her.

The late afternoon silence was broken only by the sound of harsh breathing as three pairs of lungs struggled for air.

"I'm dead. I have to be dead." Tabitha didn't know how she was even able to string two words together. She had never felt so drained—nor so energized—in her life. Problem was the energy part was all mental. The drained part was physical.

"Nope," Jonathan said from beside her. She opened her eyes when she felt his hand on her neck. "You've got a pulse. Not dead."

"Well good, then." She thought perhaps she really wasn't dead when she found she could use her left hand to stroke Jonathan's body and her right to pet James's back.

"Squishing you," James mumbled against her neck.

"Maybe a little."

He grunted, and she understood what he meant to do. She moved her arm so he could roll off her to the bed. Then he inched in close on her right side. In a few moments she would open her eyes and begin to deal with the reality of her...new reality. But for the moment it felt too nice just lying here between the brothers Keller, the awesome buzz of afterglow settling on her.

Perspiration coated her, bringing a chill to her skin. She shivered. She sighed. She said, "I could throw something together for dinner."

"We'll order in," Jonathan said. "Pizza."

"We have a much better use of your energy in mind than cooking," James explained.

"Oh, I don't know. I'd say I was using my energy pretty damn well cooking a few minutes ago."

"Agreed. But we're not done with you yet." Jonathan's words settled over her, a comforting blanket cocooning her in warmth and humor.

"In fact," James added, "I would say we've just barely gotten started."

Tabitha closed her eyes. She felt her mouth stretching into a wide smile. They'd just barely gotten started with her *and* they were spending the night.

She made a mental note to lay in a supply of vitamins and energy drinks.

* * * *

Ed Lambert checked his reflection in the glass door, ensuring what he already knew. He'd never looked better in his life.

The suit was brand new. Even though it was hot today in this God forsaken place—who the hell in their right mind moved from Washington D.C. to Carson City, Nevada?—he'd worn the suit because he knew Tabitha was a sucker for the executive look.

He had it all figured out. The hotel he was staying at in Reno had a five star restaurant. A little wining, a little dining, and he'd have her back in no time.

He'd smooth those ruffled feathers of hers, tell her that Marcy had been a terrible mistake. He'd been practicing his 'sincerely remorseful' look in the mirror, and it was good. Damn good.

Tabitha would believe him, of course. He supposed the break-up of his marriage had been his fault, in a way. He'd been stupid to give in to temptation and bring Marcy home, to screw her.

That was a mistake he'd never, ever make again. Next time, he'd rent a room.

Once everything was back to normal, and he and Tabitha were married again, he was going to go to work on getting her to tap into that trust fund. He had a good mind to give her shit for not telling him about it in the first place. But he wouldn't, of course. At least not until he'd relieved her of a fair sized chunk of it.

He'd felt like a fool when his lawyer had told him about it, and the fact that it had been protected from the divorce proceedings by his own pre-nup. If he had known about that money…

Ed stopped, closed his eyes and inhaled deeply. He was going to be facing his ex-wife in a few minutes, so it would be best if he calmed himself.

He also needed to remind himself that in some ways, his current situation really was his own fault. He knew how to handle women—tell them they're pretty, flatter them for every little thing, buy them flowers and baubles on a regular basis. His mistake had been in not treating Tabitha the way he treated the rest of his women.

He needed to get her back. Divorcing her had caused her father to pull strings, and he'd lost his job with the Department of Justice.

Being fired put a blight on his career that was going to really stand in his way when he ran for Senator. Having a divorce in your background just made you colorful. Getting fired was something else entirely.

Even that he could overcome if he could find another job. But it had been nearly three months, and his great-uncle Hubert had told him the tap of his trust fund was going to be turned off if he didn't get working again soon.

Ed pushed away all the unpleasant thoughts. It was Wednesday afternoon, about ten minutes to quitting time. He'd timed this 'reunion' perfectly so that he could sweep Tabitha off her feet and out the door. Wine her, dine her, lay her—and his future would be assured.

Pasting his best smile in place, keeping the image of himself in the role of adored and adoring husband planted front and center in his mind, he opened the door to the office building and took the first steps toward his future.

Chapter 6

"It was kind of you to let James drive your car out to the place."

"I could see that he really wanted to. Why wouldn't I share?"

Jonathan took his eyes off the road for a moment and shot her a look to see if she realized what she'd just said. The slight color flooding her cheeks told him her words had likely been a Freudian slip.

He gave her a wide smile, then stroked his hand down her leg. He couldn't not touch her. Never in his entire life had he ever spent a night like the one just passed. None of them had gotten much sleep. Maybe they'd all go have a midday nap once they settled Tabitha in. In the mean time, he decided he could answer her question honestly.

"You say that as if it would never occur to you *not* to share. But in our experience—James's and mine—it has been just the opposite. Most women we've met and dated haven't wanted us to share much time with each other."

"I don't understand that. Why wouldn't they? I could see the bond between the two of your first off. It's very clear to me that you two are more than brothers. You're best friends."

"I don't have an answer, Tabby. It frustrated the hell out of both of us. Any woman who wanted a future with either of us would have to recognize, right from the get go, that we're more than brothers, we're twins, and we're always going to be a big part of each other's lives. And yet any time one of us or both of us became involved with a woman, it seemed the first item on her agenda was to drive a wedge between us."

"Then none of those women cared enough about either of you to simply open their eyes and look."

Jonathan relaxed. He'd *known* Tabitha would get it. He couldn't say where that knowledge had come from. Just nice, he thought, to have what he'd known confirmed in words.

They cleared the city, and James passed them at the first opportunity. He seemed to be relishing the power of the machine under his hands, for he kept increasing the distance between them.

"He loves speed and the feel of powerful horsepower under his command." Jonathan heard the smile in his voice. He loved his brother above everyone else in the world, and he didn't care who knew it. And he knew he could express that sentiment to Tabitha, and she wouldn't be threatened by it.

"You not so much?" Tabitha asked.

"I do, just my definition of both speed and horse power are slightly different. Which begs the question, do you know how to ride a horse?"

"I do. My father insisted I take riding lessons—his family came from Virginia horse country. So before you tease, I can ride western as well as English."

"Did you grow up in Virginia, then?" Jonathan knew he wasn't known as a great conversationalist, but he seemed to be able to talk with Tabitha, no problem at all.

"No, upstate New York. Then we moved to Washington when Dad joined the diplomatic corps. I spent a couple of years in London when he was assigned to the Embassy there—that was when I was twelve."

"Is he still with the State Department?"

"He is. Actually, the recent change in command made him enormously happy. He very nearly quit, but kept insisting that people of sound mind were needed if for no other reason than to counter the lunacy at the top."

"He sounds like a smart man." Jonathan recalled then what she'd said about the Porsche being a gift from her father. "He didn't care for your husband?"

"No, Dad never liked Ed. I guess he could see right off the bat what I eventually discovered, because after that first year, I didn't like him much, either."

"Why did you marry him, then?"

Tabitha looked out the window for a moment before turning to face him. "I got blindsided. He presented a pretty good package. He knew just how to treat a woman to make her feel special. I had stars in my eyes, and suffered a weak moment. So I married him. But as time wore on, I began to see that it was all superficial with him. He thought he was better, smarter, more entitled to everything than I was. He wanted me to dress pretty and as I held onto his arm smile adoringly up at him. And then he cheated—with someone I believed to be a friend. Even then we probably might have saved our marriage—I do believe in second chances—if he hadn't let slip in the heat of the moment that he really had no respect for me at all. I was just a tool to him. Seems he got it in his head that when my daddy passes on, I'm going to be an heiress, rolling in money. He wanted to get his hands on that money, and *that* is why he married me. Well, that, and he had it in his head he could control me."

Jonathan couldn't keep the smile off his face. Her sense of outrage and anger had become more apparent the further into her explanation she got.

"Sounds like a stupid bastard to me. By the way, are you? Going to be an heiress rolling in money?"

Something in the way she smiled settled in a happy place inside him. When she looked at him just like that, he felt good inside and ten feet tall.

"Well, actually, I already am. I was the only grandchild for both my maternal and paternal grandfathers, so—"

She let the sentence drop, her hands spread wide. It sounded to him as if that miserable excuse of an ex-husband hadn't seen Tabitha any clearer than he and his brother had been seen by the women they'd dated.

"And your ex didn't get his hands on any of that in the divorce?"

"Ed is a bit of a trust fund baby himself. So, he had insisted on a prenuptial agreement, and my father insisted it be quid pro quo. Just for appearances sake, he'd assured Ed."

Jonathan laughed. "Your dad sounds like a good man to have around."

Tabitha sent him another winning smile. "I think so, too."

* * * *

James was leaning against the Porsche as Jonathan navigated the pickup truck toward the house.

"Look at that smile," Jonathan said as he pulled the truck to a stop just a few feet from her car.

Tabitha wondered how anyone would miss the fact that these twins genuinely loved each other. She laughed and said, "He looks as if he's hooked. You may find your truck traded in for something small, red and fast."

"Naw. He might just go out and buy one, but he'd never trade in old Betsy here." He patted the dashboard of the truck.

"What did you guys do, stop off to see the scenery? I've been waiting for hours!"

"Well, minutes, anyway," Tabitha said. "You don't strike me as the kind of man who would break the rules by speeding...overmuch."

"Guilty. Okay, let's get your stuff inside. Then we'll nag Mary into giving us lunch. *Then* we'll take you on the nickel tour."

"Tour of the house?"

"No, of the ranch."

They gave her the largest of the three guest bedrooms—although they made it clear she wouldn't be spending much time alone in it. She tested the mattress on the king sized bed. It felt sturdy enough to handle them all and the action they were bound to get into.

Tabitha didn't know what to expect from them in front of other people, but found their teasing, laughing banter very easy to take.

Mary welcomed her nicely, and had lunch waiting for them when they entered the kitchen.

"It's no one else's business what we do behind closed doors," Jonathan said quietly when she asked about how her presence on the ranch would be seen, and how it would be represented. "And besides, most of the time not even Mary—who has been with us for years—can tell us apart. Everyone here more or less treats us like one person."

They were on their way to the barn when he made that startling announcement. Tabitha stopped in her tracks, shocked.

"You said something like that once before. You mean to tell me that neither of you is treated like an individual?"

"It's all right," James said, his voice soothing. "Really. When we were younger we used to wear separate colors all the time so people *could* tell us apart. I'd wear blue mostly and Jonathan would wear brown. But we got tired of that, and tired of telling everyone which one of the Keller twins we were all the damn time."

"It's not all right. What, is everyone else *blind* around here?" She didn't have any trouble distinguishing between the two of them. What was wrong with everyone else?

They treated her to twin smiles of delight. James swooped in for a quick kiss, followed by Jonathan.

"Come on, woman," the latter said. "Let's ride."

The horse they chose for her was a beautiful chestnut mare named Aurora. She had just a tiny white patch on her head. Tabitha could see intelligence in the animal's eyes. She loved horses. It was one of the reasons she'd been happy to transfer to Carson City—so she could take a larger, more active role in the Wild Horse and Burro program.

"She used to roam wild. She was lassoed in the round up two years ago, and we adopted her." Jonathan told her. He helped her saddle the horse, and Tabitha sensed he was watching to assure himself she did know what she was doing, and how to ride. She couldn't blame him for that one bit.

"She's beautiful." Taking the time to pet the animal, she also watched the men saddle their own mounts. Their actions were smooth, practiced. Looking at them now she couldn't imagine either one of them off the range for long, yet James had seemed as at home in the casino as he was here.

"We thought we'd take a slow ride. We could talk about…things." James's announcement brought color to her face.

"I'm not used to that," she said. Placing her left foot in the stirrup, she pulled herself up and onto the mare. It had been too long since she'd ridden.

"What aren't you used to? Having two lovers at the same time?"

"Obviously. I'm not used to talking about sex, either."

"Fair enough. But you need to understand here, darlin', sex is just where we're starting. It's sure as hell *not* where we're finishing."

She knew her mouth was hanging open. Since neither one of them seemed inclined to say anything more, she had no choice but to urge her horse to follow them.

* * * *

"That shut you up," James said. They'd slowed their horses and now he and his brother flanked Tabitha. "We told you we were playing for keeps. Just what did you think that meant?"

"Think? You think I could think? I was creaming my panties. I wasn't *thinking* at all."

James looked over at his brother. Jonathan's eyes glinted in a way that told him her comment had instantly aroused him, too.

"Don't do that, darlin'. Riding a horse while I have an erection is one definition of torture," James said.

"Though it wouldn't be so torturous if that erection was buried in a hot, wet pussy," Jonathan mused.

"Damn it, now you're getting *me* horny," she complained

Tabitha looked at him, then at his brother. When she sighed, she seemed to deflate just a little. "I'm confused. Last night was the best night of my entire life. I didn't know I could have that many orgasms in one night and survive. And I have no idea what in hell I'm doing here, or what comes next. No pun intended."

"I think this is one of those situations in life where we write the rules as we go along."

James had to give his brother credit. He tended to be the quiet sort, but he was a thinker.

"Last night was the first test. I didn't know how I would feel, watching my brother fucking the same woman I'd just had myself. I wanted this, but deep down I was more than a little worried that I'd be jealous. We've shared a lot of things, but we'd never shared a woman before. I was also worried that even though this was something we both believed we wanted, that when we got naked, the three of us, it would feel…wrong. But I felt neither jealous nor…dirty. It turned me on, sharing you. And it made me feel as if everything was right, because you gave Jonathan so much pleasure."

"Yeah, that about sums it up," Jonathan said quietly. "Now what we need to know, darlin' is how you felt. How did you feel fucking two men at the same time?"

"Well, technically, I didn't fuck you both at the same time."

Her voice had come out husky, her breathing had hitched. James bet her pussy was soaking wet and ready to be plundered. Scanning the horizon, there was nothing but open range, mountains and sky. Of course, he did have that blanket strapped on the back of his saddle.

"Don't worry, darlin'. You will. But that's something we have to prepare you for. So beyond the technicality?"

They'd stopped their horses. Now he and Jonathan both turned their mounts so they could see their woman's face.

"I felt wild. Wanton. And for the first time in my life I felt…sexy. Desirable."

"Darlin', that sorry son-of-a-bitch you used to be married to ever shows his face around here, we're going to have to punch his lights out."

James smiled because his brother had said it before he could.

"You are sexy and desirable. And in about five minutes we're going to prove it to you. Again."

"Oh, yeah? What happens in about five minutes?"

There was a teasing light in her eyes, and James could see her nipples poking beneath her shirt.

"In about five minutes, we're going to reach a fence line and a tree. There, we're going to tie up our horses, spread out this blanket I've got tied to my saddle, and maybe we'll tie up you, too."

"I like the sound of that," Jonathan said. "In fact, there's a lot of things I've heard about over the years that I wouldn't mind trying, Tabby-cat, if you're feeling adventurous."

James smiled because once more his brother had voiced his very own thoughts. And it pleased him enormously that Tabitha looked even hornier than she had a few minutes before.

She glanced at Jonathan, then shook her head. "It's always the quiet ones you have to look out for."

"That didn't sound like a 'no,'" James said.

"Damn right that wasn't a 'no.' So where's this fence line and tree, gentlemen?"

James smiled. It was a good thing he and his brother had both stuffed some condoms in their pockets.

"Why, darlin', you sound downright eager."

"Yak, yak, yak," Tabitha replied. The look she sent him raised his arousal even higher. "I thought cowboys were supposed to be men of action. Less talk. More fucking."

"A woman after my own heart," Jonathan said.

Tabitha looked at Jonathan, and then him, and her gaze was aimed right at his cock.

"That isn't the body part I'm aiming for."

"I guess the only thing left to say," James laughed, "is head 'em up and move 'em out."

Chapter 7

Was there anything more arousing than standing naked before two handsome, horny men?

Well, yes, Tabitha thought in the next instant. Standing naked before two handsome, horny men while she was tied to a tree.

Her arms were stretched over her head, her wrists tied together with some rope Jonathan had attached to his saddle. They'd taken the time, and the care, to wrap her T-shirt around her wrists first, so the rope wouldn't abrade her flesh. Then they'd flung the rope over a fairly low branch, pulling it tight, raising her arms so that she stood before them, a ritualistic offering.

"This is giving me ideas. Scenarios from all the magazines I've read over the years…for intellectual content, of course." Jonathan's words washed over her in a tone that promised untold delights.

"I never before understood the appeal of having a lover, naked, bound for my pleasure. But I'm beginning to understand it."

James's voice had an equal effect on her. A slight breeze drifted past, chilling the already wet folds between her legs.

She'd never been naked outside before. James and Jonathan both seemed unconcerned about anyone coming upon them, but the thought lay in the back of her mind that they were tempting fate and that they might be discovered. The extra salacious shiver of delight that thought birthed tickled her.

"When we get home, I want to shave your pussy," Jonathan said.

The way he looked at her in that moment made her tingle. He stood beside his brother, both of them fully dressed. . Tabitha turned her gaze for one moment to the blanket the men had laid out about ten feet away on her left.

"Always in a hurry," James commented, flashing a huge grin when she flicked her gaze back to him. "Must be from working in 'the Beltway.' We do things in a more laid back fashion around here."

"You need to slow down, darlin'. Enjoy the moment. Maybe we'll try some of that tantric sex I've been reading about."

James turned his smile on Jonathan. "Yeah. We'll touch and tease and keep her *just* on the edge of orgasm for hours on end."

"You may wake up to a similar situation, you know," Tabitha warned. In fact, she just might try tying up one of them—or both of them—and see if it thrilled her as much as her current situation seemed to be doing to them.

"Perhaps. But for the moment, you appear to be all ours for the taking." James stepped closer. His smile full of the devil, he reached out and used the back of his hand to stroke the underside of her right breast.

"So incredibly soft there. Your breasts are delicious, so tasty and so very sensitive."

Jonathan came to a stop just on her left. He mimicked his brother's action. The touch, light, tantalizing, puckered both of her nipples and triggered a roll of her hips. More of her body's juices flowed.

"They do taste delicious," Jonathan agreed. Bending forward, he licked the nipple that had tightened so coquettishly for him.

"Mmm." She couldn't keep silent when if felt as if his tongue was electric, setting her blood to a steady sizzle.

"We want to play with you, Tabby-cat," James whispered. He stroked the underside of her breast again, only this time he trailed his fingers down her front, then over to rub just above her mound.

"We'll make shaving you a daily ritual. We'll take turns every morning. One of us will hold you in the shower, the other will glide the steel across your flesh. Sound good?"

"Yes. I've never showered with a man."

Jonathan smiled. "The bed isn't the only extra large appointment in your room. The attached bath has a big Jacuzzi tub and a shower large enough to hold a party in. Which we plan to do."

"Oh, yeah? Just a couple of party animals, are you?"

"Well, we're fixing to have us a party in your pussy in just a few minutes. Now, hush."

They were two separate men, but when they got that look in their eyes, it seemed they were on the same wavelength. Jonathan moved around behind her. And then they put their hands on her.

Her breasts were stroked, palms, fingers, a gossamer touch that teased then fled, returned and lingered. James's strong fingers plucked her nipples, pulling them, the pressure just on the threshold of pain. Erotic and exotic, the sensation electrified, sending sizzling strings of heat along the wire that seemed to run from her tits to her pussy.

Behind her, Jonathan stroked his hands down her back, his fingers stretching out along the sides of her breasts, dipping to the front of her to brush the hair on her pubis, then sliding back to cup and squeeze the cheeks of her ass.

"You have so many different textures, Tabitha. All soft, but different. I'll bet the flavors vary, too."

He brushed her hair aside and gave her an open-mouthed sucking kiss on the side of her neck, just where her neck connected to her shoulder.

The wet heat was duplicated as James bent forward and took her right nipple into his mouth. His sucking felt so strong, Tabitha wondered if he wanted her entire breast in his mouth. Lips and tongue pleasured her as one sly hand slowly crept down. Long male fingers combed through the blonde hair at the juncture of her thighs. Combed through, then kept their stroke slow and steady as they teased her labia.

"Spread your legs for my brother," Jonathan whispered. Tabitha could only obey. He moved his mouth along the back of her neck, tasting shoulder blades on a slow, deliberate motion that had her nearly begging. She caught his motions out of the corner of her eye as he stuck his index finger in his mouth and sucked it.

Then she felt the wet stroke of his finger against her anus.

"Oh, God!" The explosion of arousal flooded her. No lover had ever touched her there, and the urge to push back was irresistible.

"Oh, darlin', you like your ass played with, do you? We're going to have so much fun. I can hardly wait until I can fuck your ass with my cock. You'll be hot and tight around me. I'll keep thrusting in you till you scream in pleasure." Jonathan's whispered words stoked her fires and stole her breath.

"You turned her on. Her hungry little pussy clenched my fingers and then drenched them. I think I can get three of them inside her now."

A finger stroked up and down over her anus, causing her inner muscles to grip and release as if trying to grab an elusive lover. Fingers thrust into her pussy, in and out in a relentless rhythm, reaching high to tease her g-spot while at the same time a thumb caressed her clit. Up and down, back and forth, her arousal climbed and climbed.

"More!" She had to beg, because she felt so close, so very close to coming. She just needed a tiny bit more.

As one they stepped away from her, depriving her of their wickedly sensual touch.

"But we're remiss. We should strip, too."

"Damn it!" Tabitha didn't mind if they knew she felt desperate.

James chuckled at the frustration he could likely hear in her curse. Jonathan leaned in close and sent a puff of hot breath over her ear when he said, "Patience, Tabby-cat."

He walked around in front of her to join his brother, and together they began to undress. Tabitha had never been left so strung out. Her hands weren't even free to pleasure herself. She tried pulling her legs together, rubbing them close to stimulate her clit, to spark the flames of her passion, to *come*.

"Ah, ah. No cheating. The pleasure of making you come is going to be ours, Tabby-cat."

"You're always calling me that. No one has ever called me that. *Hurry*."

"We call you that for a very good reason," Jonathan said as he dropped his shirt and toed off his boots. "Because you're our very own private pussy."

She couldn't decide which one of them to watch. They were absolute studs, and both of them so hard she found it amazing they could tease her so patiently.

Whenever Ego Ed had been hard he'd needed to get his rocks off as fast as possible. Wham bam, but too self-centered to even say thank you, ma'am.

Don't think of that asshole at a time like this. Shirtless, the Kellers were impressive. Totally naked, she thought they might just be enough to make her come from simply watching them and nothing more. She waited, eagerly, to feast her eyes on them naked again.

Jonathan took the time to pull the belt from his pants, making the motion a tease in and of itself.

The sight of the leather in his hands, the way he stroked it before tossing it on the ground wrung a groan from somewhere deep inside her.

"The sight of that belt in my hands excited you? Maybe I'll turn you over my knee, lay the flat of my hand across your naked ass a few times. I won't use my belt on you, baby. I won't hurt you like that even if you beg," Jonathan said.

"I read an article once," James said as he lowered his zipper, "that claimed a little bit of pain enhanced sexual arousal. I'm all for paddling your sweet little ass to see if that's true."

"Ah, look at the way your eyes just glazed as James said that. You want that spanking, Tabby-cat."

Did she? As late as yesterday she would have sworn that the idea of any man spanking her would not only *not* have turned her on, it would have pissed her off.

The image that had formed in her mind, being laid across Jonathan's knee—or James's—and being spanked did nothing but turn her on even more.

These men are turning me into a hedonist!

James stood before her, completely naked, his cock fully erect. She wished her hands were free so she could reach out, stroke it.

He began to step toward her, then walked around so that he brushed up against her back. She could feel the silky heat of his stiff rod on her ass. Just as she tried to push back against him, to feel more of that wonderful cock against her, he took hold of her hips and held her still.

"Your nipples taste very sweet, darlin'," Jonathan said slowly. She swung her gaze to him. He was also gloriously naked, fully aroused, and had his eyes focused on her mons. "Makes me wonder what your pussy tastes like. Think I'm going to find out. Right now."

He gave no more warning than that. Falling to his knees, he put his arms between her legs to open her just a little bit more, then set his mouth on her.

Her fires had cooled, but the moist heat of his mouth shot her to the verge of orgasm. While his lips savored and slid, his tongue slicked out, swirling, stabbing into her and sucking out her essence. Satiny hot, his mouth drank her, his intimate kiss merciless, the heat and arousal so huge Tabitha had trouble catching her breath. Up, up, and over, her senses flung her into a thrilling climax. She felt the scream tear through her as the storm of orgasm battered her, relentless rapture cascading through her until she could only whimper and shake.

He grabbed her when he rose from his knees to his feet, like a god rising from the fire he'd created in her. When had they untied her? She didn't know, couldn't think. He carried her, laid her down, then thrust his cock into her, burying himself to the hilt, slamming against her cervix.

"Come for me again, woman. I want to feel your cunt milk me."

"Oh God, I can't." Had she thought Jonathan the more passive of the brothers? He was ruthless in his mastery of her, his thrusts hard and fast and deep, his determination as rigid as his cock.

"You can. You will. Here, let me share your flavor with you. Taste your juices on my lips." His words brushed her mouth and then those wicked, wanton lips gave her back her own serum in an oral assault that totally drained her will, so that all she wanted was to take whatever this stunning satyr gave her, offer all that she was to his pleasure.

Her fires re-ignited, the conflagration fanned by the heat of Jonathan's loving. Wrapping arms and legs around him, she ground her hips into his, the need to get closer, to merge, a fever inside her.

"You're hot and tight, Tabby-cat. I feel your wonderful tunnel grabbing me, sucking me in. Squeeze me, baby. Use your pussy muscles and squeeze me…yeah, like that. Come for me. Come for me now."

"Jonathan!" He had scooped her closer, his cock rubbing against her g-spot, the hair around his cock brushing her clit, and his tongue forcing her own cream into her mouth.

Her second orgasm catapulted her beyond pleasure, beyond rapture into a sphere of ecstasy so brilliant, so consuming, that she was certain she would never survive. Her heart pounded in her chest, the pulsations spreading through her body as loud as the trumpets of heaven. If this was all, if this was the end, she knew she would be content. Never had she soared, never had she relished as she did now.

If she died right this moment they would never get the smile off her face.

A solid weight pinned her down so that she knew she lived. A hot, heaving breath coated her neck so that she knew she wasn't alone. Far off, a bird sang, a cow mooed, and Tabitha understood that the world carried on, normal.

She was changed, somehow. The inferno of Jonathan Keller's passion had forged her brand new and different. She felt him move, felt him flop over on his back beside her, and closed her eyes.

Then a hand stroked her hair.

"My God, I've never seen anything so arousing," James's voice, impassioned, accompanied his light caress.

"I'm going to let you rest, though being a gentleman just might kill me. Roll over, darlin'. I'm going to rub your back and see what I can do to stoke your fires once more."

The look of longing, of pride in James's eyes nearly undid her. Jonathan had moved over, rolled over, removed the condom he'd worn and watched them, his cock now nearly flaccid.

And Tabitha wondered if, while watching her making love to James, Jonathan would become aroused again. Could someone actually be fucked too much?

She'd never believed herself capable of even a modicum of arousal, of being able to inspire more than a little interest in a lover. In two short days she'd come to know that she really didn't know what she was capable of at all.

She became determined to explore these new possibilities to their fullest. And if it killed her, she'd die happy.

"I don't need to rest, James. I need you. Kiss me. Fuck me. Make me scream."

"God, darlin'. I'll do all of that. All of that and more."

Chapter 8

Up until that day, there were only two things in Jonathan Keller's life that could move him on the deepest of emotional levels: his brother, and his land.

Now as they headed back to the ranch he realized another person had that power over him—the woman he and James had decided to call their own.

He couldn't explain why Tabitha Lambert got to him the way she did. But he knew, as he nudged his horse to catch up to them that he was already completely in love with her.

He'd never felt the kind of total completion he'd just experienced inside Tabitha's body. More than physical, their joining had rocked the foundation of his soul. Just as he would never be whole without James in his life, he knew he'd never be whole, now, without Tabitha.

He wanted to give her something and he knew the perfect gift.

"Let's take a bit of a detour," he announced.

As always, the look in James's eyes told him his brother understood.

"Good idea," he said.

"Detour to where?" Tabitha asked.

She looked like she could use a long hot bath and a nap. He figured between the two of them, he and James had worn her out. It was their duty, then, to see she got the opportunity to relax. The detour he had in mind would only add an extra twenty minutes to their ride. He was pretty certain Tabitha would count it time well spent.

"You'll see," he answered cryptically. He smiled in response to her puzzled expression.

After only a few more minutes the hillock came in view. If Tabitha had been paying attention as they'd ridden from the point where they'd left the main trail to here, she would have noticed the slow upward rise in the land. But she'd been chatting with James, and been distracted.

He wondered if his brother hadn't done just that on purpose.

Jonathan clicked at his horse, Shiloh, who responded with a puff of air and then burst into a lope. He reached the high point of land just ahead of the other two. He wanted to watch Tabitha's face as she discovered their surprise.

Her gaze was on him as she approached and he said, "You work to protect them. I thought you'd like to see them."

He noted the exact moment she caught sight of what dwelled in the valley below.

There, spanning half the length of the valley, a herd of wild horses grazed and played, roamed and rested. The herd numbered around forty. They were all colors, some small foals, some yearlings, and some more mature horses. They were, to his mind, as much a symbol of his country as was the bald eagle, or the Stars and Stripes.

"My God, they're magnificent! Just look at them! Oh, listen to them! It sounds as if they're communicating!"

"I've often thought they must say the same thing about us," he said.

He loved the way Tabitha laughed. Her eyes were alight with joy as she gave herself completely to the pleasure of watching the horses. He looked over at James, and saw the same satisfaction on his twin's face that he felt in his own heart.

"I've only ever seen pictures before, and the few video tapes that some of the field teams have taken. It's so much better seeing them like this. There's a raw energy surrounding them, as if they're a force of nature itself. Can you feel it?"

"This is a small herd. The largest one I've ever seen numbered around a hundred and twenty. When a herd that size begins to run, you can feel the vibration of their hooves hitting the ground in your belly."

"I can imagine." She sat back in her saddle. "I've been fascinated by these animals since I first heard about them when I was a child. I felt devastated when I discovered that these aren't truly 'wild' horses, as they're descended from animals that were at one time domesticated."

"That's right," Jonathan said. "They're actually 'feral' horses. Most species of wild horse are extinct now."

"Just thinking about that breaks my heart. Is this some of the land you're setting aside for them?"

"It is," James said. He pointed ahead and off slightly to the left. "Do you see those trees over at the edge of the valley? There's a stream runs through the land right there, so there's a basic source of fresh water for them. Even in the worst drought, there's usually still some water in that stream. We're close enough that, if necessary, we can run irrigation out to it. The grass is plentiful, but again, if necessary, we could deliver feed."

"That's quite an undertaking. You plan on hiring students from the university to monitor the animals?"

"We hire kids every year and give them internships," Jonathan said. "These are students enrolled in courses tied to ranching, animals or forestry, so their work becomes part of their schooling. We still pay them, of course. This will just be another learning venue for them."

Tabitha sighed as she turned her attention back to the horses. "Thank you for showing them to me. I hope I'll get plenty of opportunities to see them again."

"Count on it."

"Let's head back to the house. Darlin', you look plumb tuckered out," James said that dead-pan, and Jonathan felt honor bound to join in the teasing.

"Reckon it's because she's from the city and all," Jonathan added. "Too much riding when she's not used to it."

"Reckon," James agreed.

"It has nothing to do with being from the city and you both know it," Tabitha scoffed. Then she proved how well she fit in with them when she added, "It's the altitude."

* * * *

"I can unsaddle my own horse." That was, in fact, one of the things both her riding instructor and her father had always insisted upon. If you're going to ride, then you care for your own mount. Her father had especially been adamant that she not turn into a 'pampered miss,' so the protest came naturally when first Jonathan, then James, told her to go up to the house and leave her horse to them.

"Of course you can. But why wouldn't you allow us to see to it this once, as a favor?" Jonathan asked.

"Especially since it's our fault you're so exhausted in the first place?" James added, his voice low.

They'd dismounted close to the saddle barn. There were men about, busy doing myriad things. Tabitha could see one horse being exercised, another being bathed. A pick-up truck seemed to be in the process of being loaded with used straw.

All round her the sight of industry added to her tiny, fledgling guilt born from the idea of turning over her horse to these men and doing what she longed to do—have a long hot bath and then go to bed for a nap.

She turned to give in before that guilt grew to unmanageable proportions and noticed a black and white car coming down the lane toward the house.

"You've got company."

Both men followed her gaze. Whoever was in the cop car, neither brother seemed displeased by the arrival.

The driver must have seen them too, because rather than pulling in at the house he headed toward them.

The man who got out of the car was of average height, angular, and sporting reddish hair beneath his hat. He had an easy grin and a lazy gait. As he reached them, he pulled off his sunglasses.

"James. Jonathan." His smile was wide as he turned his attention to Tabitha, who offered her own smile in return. The man might be wearing a sheriff's deputy's uniform, but he seemed friendly enough.

"I like it when I see them together. I don't have to ask for I. D. to know who I'm talking to."

James and Jonathan both laughed. Tabitha felt herself bristling and knew she had to work on her resentment. She would have thought a trained officer of the law could at least see the differences between these two men. *My goodness, she could tell the difference and no one had ever accused her of being overly observant.*

Likely in response to the arrival of the cop car, a couple of the hands came forward and ended the discussion on horse tending by relieving all three of them of their mounts. Tabitha turned her attention back to James when he said her name.

"Tabitha," he placed his hand on her back, stroked once. "This is a good friend of ours, Derek Hamilton. He's Deputy Hamilton these days. Derek, Tabitha Lambert."

Tabitha offered her hand. For a man of the law the deputy had a limp, clammy handshake.

"Ms. Lambert."

"Deputy." It took some effort to give the man a friendly smile. She was going to have to work on accepting the fact that, for whatever reason, no one else seemed able to tell James and Jonathan apart.

"Thought I'd stop by, give you a 'heads up.' We've had some reports of suspicious activity in the area. People spotted who don't belong, some unmarked transport trucks, that sort of thing."

"You think we've got illegals smuggling in the area?" Jonathan asked.

"Illegal what?" Tabitha wanted to know.

"People," James replied.

"Not sure. There have been rumors about some gang incursions into the northern part of the state here for the last few months. So far, they've been only rumors. We don't see as much of that sort of thing in Nevada as they get in Arizona and California. But we get some, and any rumblings bear investigation."

"I'll check with the men, see if they've noticed anything. You don't think it could be rustlers?" Jonathan asked. To Tabitha he said, "We had some cattle go missing about ten years ago, when the price of beef was high. Finally caught the bastards."

"At this point, we have no idea even if anything is really going on, or what it could be. Drugs, people, cattle or horses. Take your pick. So I'll be taking a few shifts on horseback in the next little while. Just wanted to let you know in case you saw me riding your land and wondered why."

"Hell, Derek, you're always welcome here," Jonathan said.

The deputy's words finally registered with her. "Horses? Someone might be stealing horses? I'll want to know if that's what's happening. That would be a federal matter."

When the deputy tilted his head at her comment, James explained, "Tabitha is with the BLM, the Wild Horse and Burro program."

"Is that so?" Deputy Hamilton seemed surprised by that information, and Tabitha wondered if he was one of those throw-backs she encountered every once in a while—the kind who believed certain professions were for the major testosterone-makers only.

"It is." She looked at Jonathan. "How long until we get that refuge set up and under surveillance?"

"Refuge?" the deputy asked.

"The Kellers are designating a portion of their lands to serve as a wild horse refuge. They're underwriting the cost of having it monitored and maintained, as well. I'm very excited about it. Once it's set up, you'll have even more people in the area who can be your eyes and ears, Deputy."

"Well, that's certainly generous of you boys."

Tabitha couldn't contain her smile. Her two strong, manly lovers were blushing! James shot her a look then turned to the deputy.

"Anything we can do to lend a hand with your investigation, be sure to let us know. In the meantime, we'll talk to the crew, see if they've encountered anything."

"Appreciate that. I'd also appreciate that if they report anything you let me know about it right away. Don't take any actions yourself. If it is something bigger—like drug or people smuggling—we'd want to observe for a time before taking action."

"Don't worry," Jonathan said. "We'll leave the hero work to you."

"There you go. Boys. Ma'am."

He tipped his hat to her then turned and walked back to his car.

"Is there a lot of crime in this area, then?" she asked as they watched the vehicle drive out of sight.

"Not really," James said. "But there's some."

"Being a deputy seems to suit Derek," Jonathan said as they began to walk toward the house.

It was late afternoon and the temperature hovered in the high eighties. Tabitha felt the heat, though she was quite aware it didn't feel anywhere near as hot here in this arid region as it would have back east.

"It does," James agreed. "Maybe he's finally found his place."

"So you know him quite well?" she asked, as they mounted the steps.

"Yeah, all our lives. He's always been a bit of a loner. Never married. Never even dated much, come to that," Jonathan held the door open for her. "He worked with us here a few summers, but I don't think we were ever really close friends. He always seemed to hold himself back, to not quite fit in."

"His mom was our fourth grade teacher. His dad's worked construction for years. Takes pride in his work. The Hamiltons are good people."

"It's always been my opinion that there are more good people in the world than the cynics would have us believe."

"That's pretty much been our opinion, too," James said.

He ran his hand down her back again. Jonathan put a hand on her left shoulder and squeezed gently.

"Why don't you go have a nice hot bath? Dinner won't be read for a few hours. One of us will be up in a bit to…wash your back," James said.

"Only one of you?" A part of her wanted to stand back and shake her head. She never knew she could pout quite so well.

"It's time for a little one on one attention, don't you think?" Jonathan asked.

"Remember," James added, dead pan, "variety is the spice of life."

Tabitha laughed. "Yeah, like my life isn't nice and spicy right now, just as it is." Then she felt her smile sober. "I'm still having trouble wrapping my head around us." She looked at each man in turn and was offered twin expressions of understanding.

"Around the reality of having two lovers at the same time? It's enough to confuse any woman, I'm sure," James said. "That's why we both think we need one-on-one time."

"No," she replied as she headed toward the stairs and a soak in that big, deep Jacuzzi. It was probably a mistake on her part to admit anything more. She'd always been accused of wearing her heart on her sleeve. Maybe she'd scare them off with the words she was going to give them. But she believed in being honest, and she didn't want these men to think even for one moment that she was letting her pussy do her thinking for her.

"What I'm having trouble wrapping my head around is that I have discovered that I could very easily fall in love with both of you."

Twin looks of shock, twin smiles of dawning joy were her reward for her candor. Then she headed for her room, and that soak.

Chapter 9

"That was one hell of an exit line."

Tabitha lay looking sweet and serene, her eyes closed, as the Jacuzzi jets swirled frothy water over her body. He watched as her eyes opened, as she focused on him and smiled.

He'd come into the bedroom, heard the jets from the adjoining bath and stripped. He'd set a couple of thin packets down by the edge of the tub. Now he stood naked, watching her.

"James. Are you just going to stand there, or are you going to join me?"

"Do you know," he confessed as he stepped into the tub, "the fact that you can tell us apart—something that baffles the hell out of us both, by the way—turns me on enormously. Jonathan, too."

Tabitha frowned, and he thought the look adorable. Rather than impale her immediately as a part of him longed to do, he lounged against the edge of the tub directly across from her. Opening his legs, he reached down and picked up her left foot, lifted it and brought it between his knees.

"It ticks me off that no one can tell you apart. I mean, yeah, you look a lot alike, but you're not identical. I could see the differences between you the day we met, and I'm not a particularly observant person." She sounded aggrieved on his behalf—and Jonathan's—and that just made his heart melt a little bit more.

"Actually, love, we are. Identical twins, not fraternal."

"Oh."

He'd begun massaging the bottom of her foot and he could see the effect he was having on her. Her eyes glazed, and he knew she'd lost the edge of the conversation. In the next moment she gave a long, lustful groan as she tipped her head back, closed her eyes and slid a little bit deeper into the water.

"That feels *wonderful*."

"Glad to hear it. So, by the way, do you."

"So do I do what?" Her eyes were still closed, her tone distracted.

"Feel wonderful. Physically, when I have my cock buried deep inside you. Emotionally when I watch my brother fucking you and see the way you wrap around him and the pleasure you get and the look of heaven on his face."

"The two of you are turning me into a hedonist, a voluptuary when I believed I was right next door to frigid. I've never experienced such good orgasms in my entire life. I never believed I could."

"Darlin', you're as far from frigid as it's possible to get. Trust me. I know. Personally, I am more pleased than I can say that you get hot for me and for Jonathan in equal measure. You respond to us instantly and completely in a way I had longed for, but never really believed would ever happen."

He worked his hands up her calf, smoothing and kneading the tension from her body. They hadn't gone that far today, but it had been far enough for someone not yet used to riding.

Hell, she'd been ridden hard since the night before when he stopped and thought about it.

"If you stop, I may have to murder you."

Laughter rumbled from his chest and it felt good. "Oh, I'm not going to stop, darlin'. But I will change legs."

"Mmm. Another time when Jonathan joins us maybe I can get *both* legs done simultaneously."

"You can count on that."

He made good on his promise, set her left leg back under the water and reached for her right. Her skin was soft and silky, the muscle well toned. Touching her—even so nearly innocent a touch as this, made his cock harden. She sighed again, and opened her eyes into little slits, just enough that she could see him.

She raised her right foot and gently stroked his erection. "I love the feel of your cock. It's so hot and hard, yet when I stroke it I feel the delicate texture of the skin. And I want to taste it, to feel it in my mouth, caress it with my tongue as I suck on it."

Her words inflamed him. "You certainly give as good as you get, darlin'. Verbally as well as physically."

"Which is a surprise to me. I was married." She looked at him and he could see the vulnerability she tried to hide. "It turned out to be a mistake. But for a while, I tried. He never made me feel half as good as you and Jonathan make me feel."

"Roll over and get on your knees, darlin'. I'm about to make you feel a whole hell of a lot better than good."

He loved that siren's smile of hers. Enjoying the view, he relaxed and watched as her luscious body rose from the foam. *A water nymph, just waiting to play.* It was a fanciful thought for a man who considered himself grounded in the realities of the twenty-first century. Then she was on her knees. When she looked back, tossing him that saucy come-fuck-me look over her shoulder, he nearly just dove forward and into her.

But he really wanted to play, first. He reached down to the floor for one of the foil packets he'd tossed there. Rising from the water he donned the latex quickly.

He scooped up the bar of soap, a flowery bit of compact silk that spread lather on his hands as he rubbed them together. Then his hands were on her skin and the sensation aroused them both. Sliding, he worked his way from the small of her back to her shoulders. One knee was braced on the bench between hers, and his cock stroked up and down the crack of her ass as he massaged the lather in.

"Oh, God, that feels good."

"You want more?"

"Please."

He reached around, his hands cupping, fondling, squeezing her breasts. He knew he'd aroused her, for she was moving her ass against his cock. Her nipples had turned into rigid buttons. He pinched them between thumbs and forefingers, pulling slightly.

"Have you ever taken a man's cock in your ass, honey?" The way she kept using that beautiful bottom of hers to stroke him had him nearing the point of no return. If it turned out to be something she was used to, he'd accommodate her here and now.

"Never. I never wanted to until the two of you. Will you fuck my ass?"

"You tempt me. But I won't hurt you like that, won't take you without first stretching you a little."

"You've turned me into a complete nymphomaniac. All I want is your hands and your mouths and your cocks. On me and in me. Over and over again."

"Darlin', we haven't turned you into anything, we've just brought out your hidden talents. And maybe some of ours, too. Do you recall our conversation earlier? When we had you tied up?" He leaned forward then, moving his cock so that he no longer teased her anus, but rubbed against her labia as he whispered in her ear. "I loved having you bound. I want to tie you to the bed, arms and legs, blindfold you and pleasure you till you scream. You, my lovely Tabby-cat, seem to have brought out the latent Dom in me."

"Not latent," she hissed. He moved, wouldn't allow her to capture his cock with her pussy lips. She very nearly caught him. God, she was clever. "Nothing latent about the Dom in you. I saw it the first time I laid eyes on you. It's like a mantle of power...God, *James*! Please!"

He'd moved his lather covered hand down and found her clit. He tortured them both by stroking not only her slit, but his cock as it stretched between the folds of her pussy. All he had to do was change the angle slightly and he'd be deep inside her. It was hell to deny himself, to deny them both. But he had a mind to try something new.

"We talked about spanking you. Do you remember?"

"Please…oh, James, please I *need*—"

He loved that he could reduce her to begging, and that she could in turn do the same to him. There was a freedom in that, in knowing there was safety in the needing, in the wanting.

"I know what you need, Tabitha." He continued to rub them both with one hand and waited until she whimpered once more, until she moved her hips backward trying to capture his cock.

He brought his open hand down on her naked ass.

* * * *

The sting shocked, her scream sharp and involuntary. James kept massaging her pussy, his hot cock pressing against her slit and rubbing her clit as the heat of the smack radiated out over her entire ass.

It hurt good. All she could think was *more.*

"*Oh God.*"

"Again? Yes, or no?"

Damn him for making her take responsibility for this, for showing her that she was raw and basic when she'd always believed herself refined. Her body craved, demanded, controlled. Gripping the edge of the tub she pressed herself more closely to the man-flesh that tormented her clit and tilted her ass toward him, telling him with actions instead of words that he could do whatever he wanted to her.

"Such a pretty invitation. Such a lovely ass just begging to be spanked. But I need the words, Tabby-cat. Tell me. Tell me now."

Tabitha thought she would explode into a million tiny fragments if she didn't get what she wanted, and cursed him again for making her own her actions, even as she respected—loved him for it.

"Yes, damn you, yes. Again. Please. Oh, God, James, I need—"

This slap was as hard, as sharp as the first, the sting potent, nearly cutting, as it edged her arousal beyond the known.

"Just one more." His voice sounded forced. The press of his cock against her folds intensified, as his rod became even more rigid, as the heat of it singed her.

His hand came down a third time, and Tabitha screamed, "Fuck me!" as her orgasm shot from her clit to her toes.

James swore, moved his hips and plunged into her. Tabitha pushed back against him, countering each of his pounding thrusts with demands of her own, her hips slamming back against his as the orgasm bucked through her.

She felt James's arm wrap around her from behind, felt him lean onto her. His groan as he began to ejaculate vibrated through her back, making her nipples tingle. The sensation of his cock pulsating within her pushed her over the edge once more. Rapture curled and writhed as pleasure tested the boundaries of sanity until Tabitha could only cling to the tub and gasp for air.

"Oh God, oh God," she heard the whimper and didn't care how she sounded. Surely she was destroyed, her body torn apart from the thunderbolts of ecstasy that had slammed into her. Her heart hammered in her chest as fast and hard as James's pounded against her back. She struggled to draw in lungful after lungful of breath.

Tabitha felt his lips kiss her shoulder. He withdrew his cock from her gently. She couldn't move. She heard a sound that told her he'd removed the condom. And then he was sitting down beside her, prying her fingers off the edge of the tub and turning her around, settling her into his embrace, cradling her in his arms.

"Shh. I have you, darlin'. It's all right, I have you."

Only when he wrapped her in his arms did she realize she was shivering and sobbing.

"Are you cold, baby? Did I hurt you?"

"N..no. Too much pleasure."

"You mean I fucked you into a shivering, quivering mass?"

She laughed, the whispered question holding a hint of wistfulness. But his actions, the stroking of his hands on her arms and back were infinitely tender.

"Something like that." The shivering had calmed. Exhaustion replaced the frenzied aftershocks. Unable to hold back the urge, she yawned.

James kissed the top of her head. Then he stroked a finger under her chin, lifting her face for his kiss. His lips, hot, moist, caressed and teased her own. The kiss was questing, tasting, maybe even a bit reverent.

God, Tabitha, you're getting maudlin. But she gave him all she could, her tongue loving the taste of him, the feel him. This was pleasure of another sort, and she drank of it freely.

He weaned his lips from hers. "Wait right here."

"Where would I go? Besides, I couldn't move if I had to."

"Well you won't have to. At least, not much."

She closed her eyes for what she was certain was only a moment. The sound of him calling her name roused her, but just barely.

"Come here, Tabby-cat."

She felt as if her head was stuffed with cotton, as if the sounds around her were muted by a giant filter. Opening her eyes, she saw the towel waiting for her. She only just managed to lift herself out of the water. But that was all she needed to do. He wrapped her in the heated terry. *Bliss.* She didn't even mind his chuckle when she curled into the heat, and into him. She tried to co-operate as he dried her, but function was a faculty she was quickly losing the capacity to perform.

When he lifted her, carried her, she gave herself permission to go boneless in his arms. She gasped a moment later when he laid her on the bed.

"Sorry, darlin'. You'll heat the sheets in no time."

"No energy."

His laughter teased her sense of humor, and she felt herself smile.

"No, I know. Your hot little body will heat the sheets all by itself. You need to sleep now, baby. You're exhausted. It's only five. How about a late dinner, maybe around ten? Something light like soup and sandwiches. How does that sound?"

"Ambrosia."

She lay on her stomach. Something chilly touched her back, and she felt James's hands on her, smoothing, massaging. Unlike in the tub, this touch soothed rather than aroused. The scent of peaches identified the lotion he was using as her very own.

"Sleep, baby."

That sounded like a good idea. She nearly told him so, but drifted off before she could.

Chapter 10

His anger built slowly throughout the rest of the day.

Derek knew that no one was aware of his mood, no one could see the storm that raged within him. He'd gotten very good at hiding that part of himself from everyone.

People he'd known all his life, even his own parents, thought he was an easy-going, happy-go-lucky stooge. *Assholes.*

The sun sank toward the western horizon and he seethed. How like those bastard Kellers to fuck him up just when he'd found a way to get ahead! How many years had they ignored those horses roaming these parts? Always, that's how long. Why now? Bastards, they always had something going on, some scheme to keep getting richer and richer. They were likely cheats, just like their great grandpa. That sort of thing came down in the blood. He snorted. *How like them to scheme and manipulate anyone they thought they could to come out looking pristine.*

He'd caught the way one of them had touched that BLM agent— Tabitha. Did she know they were only using her? That they would use her and then when they didn't need her any more, just toss her aside? Ignore her?

Thoughts of Tabitha Lambert distracted his anger. She was a pretty little thing with a nice smile. Her eyes had sparkled when she'd looked up at him. The sunlight had played off her golden hair. She'd looked like a princess.

Derek didn't think she'd looked at either one of those Kellers quite the same way as she'd looked at him. She'd been polite to them, of course. And had praised their generosity. Likely, working for the government and having been sent out by her boss, she'd have been under orders to suck up. He'd gotten similar orders himself in the past. Sucking up always left a rotten taste in his mouth.

Derek would bet Tabitha Lambert felt the same way. In fact, he'd be willing to bet that he and Tabitha Lambert had a great deal in common, could connect on several different levels.

He paced the small kitchen in his apartment, his gaze drawn to the world outside the window—to the hills and rolling fields and mountains in the distance. His folks owned a squat piece of that land, and to listen to them talk, you'd think it was a fucking estate.

He wanted better, and he wanted more. Hell, he deserved better and more, didn't he?

Those thoughts carried him through into the parlor where his computer sat, waiting. He checked his e-mail, smiling when he saw the reply he'd been hoping for.

His contact had returned the picture he'd given him, not with one horse circled, but two! He was promised a bonus if he could deliver within the next two weeks.

He could do it. He knew of a place where he could pen one horse while he caught the other. And he knew something else he could do, too.

Being a Deputy had privileges. He logged onto a site regular citizens couldn't access and conducted a search. Within minutes he had the information he sought. He'd been reasonably certain that he would have heard talk about a pretty blonde joining the ranks of the civil service in Winnemucca. But Ms. Lambert worked out of Carson City, and she was new there.

That meant her connection to the Kellers was new, too. New enough to develop a few cracks, if it was hit hard enough, and in the right place.

Maybe he really could kill two birds with one stone: enrich himself, and smear the Kellers.

After—when those bastards had been put down, when his own star was clearly in ascendancy—then he'd go after Tabitha. But first, he had a different use for her in mind. His plan would work better if he had an employee of the federal government on his side. She had a passion for those wild horses, he'd seen it in her eyes. Yes, first he would plant seeds of doubt. Then he would shock and horrify. Derek smiled, because he had sudden image of Tabitha Lambert as his very own avenging angel.

He was tired of seeing those two golden boys cruise through life looking like heroes. It was time they wore a little dirt. And he'd use that pretty Ms. Lambert to throw it on them.

* * * *

Tabitha felt their eyes on her. She paused with her fork half-way to her mouth. Jonathan and James wore twin expressions of amazement. They were staring at her as if they'd never seen a woman eat before.

"What?"

"Um...do you eat like that *all* the time?" Jonathan asked.

"Good thing we put her in Uncle Rolly's bedroom." James observed, sotto voce.

Tabitha contained the smirk that wanted to escape. Teasing was definitely number two on the list of what these men liked to do best. Number one was the reason she was stuffing herself full of bacon, sausage, flapjacks, eggs and biscuits at seven o'clock in the morning.

"Actually, if we want to talk about voracious appetites..." She smiled her sweetest smile and batted her eyes at them.

Both men chuckled. "No, I would say the last two days were definitely not indicative of our usual...behavior," James conceded. "And since you ended up not getting anything to eat last night, I suppose we should just button it and let you enjoy."

"That might be an idea," she allowed. Since she could no longer keep her own laughter back she didn't worry that either of them had misread her mood.

The sound of music—the first few bars of the theme from Rocky—found Tabitha reaching for her purse. Her cell phone sat in its usual place—tucked into a little pocket, and was all aglow and singing merrily.

"Hello?"

"Where the hell are you?"

The unwelcome voice sent a shiver down her spine. Tabitha pulled the phone away from her ear long enough to look at the caller I.D. Her heart sank when she realized it was the Reno area code.

"Ed?"

"Well of course it's me. How many other men do you have calling you?"

There must have been something in her eyes that communicated distress, because both James and Jonathan sat up straighter, all signs of teasing gone.

"None of your business. What are you doing in Reno? And how did you get my cell phone number?"

"I've come to see you, baby-face. I was very disappointed to come all this way and then discover you were nowhere to be found. That cute little hard body manning the phones at your office said you'd taken a few days off to get settled in, but when I showed up at your house, you weren't there. The red-head who lives next to you—she's hot by the way—said she thought you drove off yesterday with someone."

"Really?" Subtlety had always been lost on Ed. Her temper was rising and the food she'd just eaten churned in her belly. She didn't realize she'd put a hand there until Jonathan got up and came over to kneel in front of her. He replaced her hand with his own.

Just that easily, her stomach settled.

"So where are you, and when are you coming back? I thought we could have a nice, quite dinner somewhere…I'll order you your favorite wine…and we can talk about all the good times we had. I've missed you, baby-face. I've missed you real bad."

"The only 'good times' we ever had began when I kicked your sorry ass out the door and filed for divorce." Both men chuckled, but did their best to cover the sound.

"Aw, now, baby-face, don't be like that. I don't blame you for being a bit irked with me. But can't we just let that nasty water flow under the bridge? I just want the chance to make it up to you. Come on, just you, me, some candle light and soft music…"

He'd dipped his voice to that intimate tone he had, the one that had hooked her in the first place. And Tabitha wondered what in hell she'd been smoking at the time that she'd even been swayed by him. Here and now, with two of the most virile men she'd even met listening in—Ed tried to talk in an intimate voice but he was unfailingly loud—she knew as never before that she must have been suffering the weak moment to end all weak moments to have ever said yes to him. She also knew, if she hadn't understood it before, that she was well and truly over him.

"Listen, Ed, I moved from DC to Nevada, clear across the damn country. Doesn't that tell you something? Like maybe I don't want to even be in the same *state* with you, never mind the same room. And furthermore—"

She stopped because James had reached over and placed his hand on her arm to get her attention. He hastily scrawled a note on a paper napkin then turned it for her to see.

She frowned at James and he winked back. Looking at Jonathan she could see he was in agreement with his twin—big surprise there. Sighing, she decided to give her lovers what they apparently wanted.

"Okay, look. We can have a drink. Aces and Jacks Casino right there in Reno. There's a lounge off the gaming floor. It's called the Double Diamond. Eight o'clock tonight."

"Baby, you won't be sorry. This is going to be a whole new beginning for us. You'll see."

He'd hung up and for a long moment Tabitha just looked at her phone.

"Of all the egotistical, delusional…"

"Did I just hear him correctly? Did your ex-husband, just now, during a phone call in which he was obviously trying to persuade you to meet him and make kissy face, tell you your neighbor was *hot*?"

Jonathan's incredulity did a lot to smooth the hackles that hearing her ex-husband's voice had raised. "Well," she said as she set the cell phone back in her purse, "I don't call him Ego Ed for nothing."

"Since we're going to be meeting the gentleman later this evening, why don't you tell us about him? And about your divorce? Unless, of course you don't want to."

How could she have lucked out to get her hands on not one but two men who seemed to *get* her? The tenderness in James's eyes, the gentleness of Jonathan's touch left her with no doubt they cared for her.

"I don't mind. The first thing you have to understand is that this situation is entirely my fault."

"Bullshit. How do you figure that?" Jonathan asked.

He must have realized her tummy had settled, for he pulled a chair closer and sat next to her, his hand occupied stroking her arm instead of her stomach.

"I'm a blue-eyed blonde." She looked from one to the other of them. They wore twin expressions of confusion.

"And?"

"Well, you know those jokes that men—and non-blonde haired women—like to pass around? About blondes?"

First James, and then Jonathan darted their eyes away as their cheeks took on a faint pinkish glow.

James was the first to laugh, outright. "Okay, we used to. But never again, I swear. Not after meeting you, getting to know you."

"Me too, darlin'. What do blonde jokes have to do with anything?" Jonathan asked.

"Well, Ed believed them. My favorite one is two blondes sitting on a park bench in New York City on a warm summer night. The moon is full and bright and one blonde asks the other, "Which do you think is closer, Miami, or the moon?" And the second blonde says, "*Hello*, can you see Miami from here?"

Tabitha had to give them credit. She saw the laughter in their eyes, caught the way they both struggled to contain it. They were men of fierce will, indeed.

Finally, they both laughed out loud. "Okay, but he couldn't have held that opinion after even five minutes in your company," James protested.

"One of the first things we noticed about you was your quick mind. And you will note I said *one* of the things, because I'm not going to lie, that is one hell of a sexy body you have on you Ms. Lambert."

"Aw, shucks." Tabitha couldn't resist. She leaned over and placed a quick kiss on Jonathan's lips. Then, of course, she did the same to James.

"And thank you for that, but I'm afraid Ed never got over that first preconceived notion about my IQ being related to my hair color, and possibly my bra size."

"I see that smile. What memory has you nearly laughing?" James asked.

"I worked for the Department of the Interior in DC while Ed was with Justice. We both had to take department ordered IQ tests—I think this was about four months after we were married. I was already beginning to have second thoughts about my decision to become Mrs. Lambert at the time. Anyway, the results were posted the same day about a week later."

"Outscored him, did you?" Jonathan asked

"One forty-two to one-twelve."

"Ouch. I'm guessing he didn't take it well?" James asked.

"He accused me of flaunting my tits to get a better score."

"Fucking moron."

Tabitha laughed, because both men had said that at the same time. Then she sobered. "I'm only going to see him tonight because you want me to, but I'm sure as hell not going alone. I meant it. I moved across the country to get away from that bastard."

Jonathan stroked her back and James picked up her right hand and kissed it. "Of course you won't see him alone. We'll both be with you. In fact, I think we could all have a lot of fun with this."

"We could stay over in the Penthouse, if you like," Jonathan offered. His smile turned up at one corner of his mouth and she knew he was going to tease her. "It has a king sized bed there, too. So we can have dinner at the all-you-can-eat buffet, no worries about anybody being crowded out of sleeping space, afterward."

"Smart ass. I really do have a good appetite—for more things than just food—just about all the time. However, I seem to also be blessed with an excellent metabolism. All my family is. But now that I think about it, you were making some not-so-*thinly* veiled references to an uncle…did you really have an uncle named Rolly?"

"Our mother's brother. He passed on, what, five years ago now?" Jonathan asked, his comment directed to his brother.

"About that," James confirmed.

"I'm sorry."

"Don't be. He was ninety-three and by his own admission had lived a hell of a good life. So to answer your question, healthy appetites run in our genes, too." Jonathan's voice dipped, and just that easily Tabitha felt moisture gathering between her legs.

"I had noticed the appetites."

"And since we're going to town it will give us the opportunity to go…toy shopping." James's voice had also dipped. His tone left her in no doubt as to the kind of toys they would be buying.

"I can't say that I've ever done that," she replied.

"Stick with us, darlin'. We'll take you places you've never been before."

Tabitha reached out with both hands. With no problem at all she was able to stroke twin hard cocks.

"You already have. And all I can say is, I seem to have discovered a latent taste for exploration."

Chapter 11

The one thing Jonathan liked best about the penthouse suite of the Aces and Jacks Casino and Hotel—aside from, in this instance, the king-sized bed—were the windows. One entire wall in the living room was floor to ceiling glass. The view year round was spectacular. In the daylight hours the mountain that lay across the valley rose majestically toward the sky, dwarfing the sprawling city beneath it and, Jonathan thought, rendering it completely inferior. But at night time the city sparkled, a million glittering lights in every color of the rainbow shimmering in the dark, more dazzling than any crown jewels. It was at night the city claimed back its stature as a wonder in the middle of the arid northern Nevada landscape.

"The view is spectacular," Tabitha said as she came to stand beside him.

"You have your voice back. I thought we'd rendered you permanently speechless."

The look she gave him was pure coquette and had his cock stirring. Not that it hadn't been begging to rise to the occasion since they'd entered that sex shop earlier.

"That was an experience," she said, a slight laugh in her voice. "I'm not sure what intrigued me the most—the fur lined handcuffs, the leather paddles, or the butt plugs."

"You left out the collar, the leash, the massage oils, and the nipple clamps." James had come up to stand beside them. Then he shot Tabitha a teasing wink. "You realize of course that we bought them all."

"You didn't! I didn't see you do that!"

"The entire time we were in there James kept taking items to the counter. When you were looking at those sexy lingerie sets, he paid for them and carted them out to the truck." Jonathan loved the way Tabitha's cheeks turned a bright pink and the sparkle that set her eyes glowing.

"And that bag is now in the bedroom. I especially like the collar we chose for you." James smiled, and Jonathan knew his brother was already thinking of the fun they would have together later tonight, once they got rid of that irritating ex-husband.

"You bought me a collar."

Jonathan sent a glance to James. They were both trying their best not to laugh.

"The terms of the wager—which you forfeited when you folded your hand—were that we would make each and every one of your fantasies come true. We're just trying to cover all the bases. Never let it be said that any Keller failed to hold up his end of a bargain," James said, and Jonathan could see he enjoyed teasing their woman.

"The collar has the words 'Bad Kitty' inscribed upon it—via silver metal studs on black leather. Oh, and there's a leash, too. Since you're our very own Tabby-cat, we figured finding that collar was kismet," Jonathan added.

Tabitha was looking from James to him. "What," she asked sweetly, "do *your* collars have inscribed on them?"

"Now there's a thought," James replied quickly. "We'll have them made specially. Probably just the word 'Master' inscribed on each."

"Short, simple, succinct. I like it," Jonathan agreed.

"That," Tabitha said through her laughter, "is going to earn you both some payback."

"Speaking of payback," Jonathan said as he reached over and ran his hand down her back, "you owe me a session in the shower. I very much want to shave you."

"Oh, boy. Water sports." She'd said that on a gasp. He flicked a look down to see her newly awakened nipples poking her shirt to get his attention.

"Yeah. I hear you indulged in some last night." He reached for her then, bringing her into his arms. James ambled over to one of the overstuffed chairs and sat down.

Funny, but they never discussed between them what they would do when they got together with Tabitha. Well, except for last night when they both decided that James would be the one to join her in her bath. Their time together, their intimacies, simply happened.

She wrapped her arms around his neck and nestled her body close to his. He loved the feel of her breasts pressing against his chest. Her mound snuggled up to his erection. It didn't take much for her to make him hot.

He combed his fingers through her hair, tilted her head back. For a long silent moment they looked into each other's eyes. He saw desire there, and understood it was desire for *him*. He'd never been a fanciful man, but he would swear he saw her soul there too, and that soul was gentle and pure and…questing. He believed that she had been yearning for them in the same way that he—and his brother—had been yearning for her.

Jonathan laid his mouth on hers, wanting to show her with his lips and tongue, with his hands caressing her back and bottom, and his arms wrapping snugly around her, how much she meant to him. He wouldn't risk the words, not yet. The time would come, he knew, to give them. Again, nothing to be planned between he and James, but he knew his brother felt the same way about her. And he knew that between them they had already decided this woman was *theirs*. Tabitha Lambert belonged to them. He supposed that was only fair since he and James belonged to her, too.

Her flavor soothed and aroused, tripped his heart and fired his blood. He swirled his tongue in her mouth, tasting every bit of her.

Through the thin barriers of cloth that separated his chest from her breasts, he felt her nipples beading.

He weaned his lips from hers. Tabitha made him want things he never knew he could crave. "Will you let me strip you? Will you let James and I take you into the shower? Will you let me shave your sweet little pussy?"

"Yes, please."

* * * *

Like the bathroom at the ranch, this one was spacious, with shower and tub both big enough to party in.

Tabitha thought Jonathan would use soap on her, but he surprised her when he brought the can of shaving foam into the shower.

"This brand has a slight numbing property to it, darlin'. If I accidentally nick you, the foam will prevent it from stinging too badly."

"I never knew that. All these years I've been using soap on my legs. I think I'll switch. Just do me a favor. Don't slice anything important off down there."

"Don't worry."

Tabitha knew she couldn't laugh. One of her lovers was standing behind her naked, holding her against him, one arm snug around her waist, the other holding up her right leg. Bent at the knee, James held it in such a way as to leave her pussy fully exposed.

Her other lover was on his knees before her wielding a razor. If she laughed, she really would be sorry. But boy, did she ever love being teased by, and teasing these two.

"Ready, darlin'?" Jonathan asked.

"Ready. Though I'm going to need fur lined panties for the winter months now."

Jonathan looked up at her and his expression was so heated she thought she'd melt. "When you're cold, you can just wear us."

How could he always inflame her with just words? "That would be an interesting look for meetings."

His grin flashed, a devil's grin. Then she felt the first glide of cold steel against her flesh. Her shiver was pure reflex.

"Careful, darlin'," Jonathan whispered. His hot breath caressed the skin newly revealed. Arousal, never completely gone, began to eddy and flow through her, the smoke of embers glowing and getting hotter.

He was slow in his movements, the caress of his tool gentle but thorough. They'd only had the water on long enough to get them all wet, and now as the air swirled around her, her flesh puckered with a slight chill.

The furnace-like heat of James behind her kept her back warm. His cock was hard and pressed against her ass, reminding her of some of the things he'd said and done the night before.

"You have such a pretty pussy, Tabby-cat. And now I can see all of it." Jonathan set the razor aside, then turned the shower on to a gentle spray. Using his hands he cupped water then released it against her belly so that it flowed over her mons, sluicing the rest of the foam away.

His rapt attention, more than the heated water, began to warm her blood.

"When I stroke you just a little like this," he suited actions to words, running the back of his fingers over her labia, back and forth. "When I do this, your luscious lips pout and your clit awakens. It sticks up it's cute little head like it's trying to catch my eye. I think they both want my undivided attention."

He set his mouth on her and Tabitha cried out, the spike in arousal so sharp her hips rolled in response. Soft, silky, hot his tongue slid over her pussy, spearing into her tunnel then out. Opening his mouth wide, he moved his lips over her in exotic, erotic motion.

"Oh, Jonathan, *yes*," she whimpered, her body gathering, chasing after the rapture his mouth promised. Her nipples beaded into hard points, and James used his fingers to pluck and pull them almost in perfect sync to the rhythm of Jonathan's tongue.

"You taste sweet, Tabitha. My own personal ambrosia."

He'd spoken against her flesh and the vibration of his words tickled her clit, the sensation causing her tunnel to clench, like a finger curling in wanton invitation.

Jonathan deftly inserted his fingers, reaching high and finding her g-spot. Then he clamped his lips around her clitoris and sucked the eager flesh into his mouth.

Her cry of pleasure erupted unrestrained. All strength left her knees as waves of orgasm washed over her, shockwaves of pleasure that consumed every atom of her being. Pleasure, seemingly unending, took up every thought, every sight, every sound. On and on ecstasy cascaded until she could only mew as she gasped for air.

When she could draw a full breath, when she could almost take her weight on her own feet, she opened her eyes. The expression of satisfaction on Jonathan's face filled her heart to overflowing.

"Okay, cowboy," she murmured. James released her and she got to her knees. Her attention focused on Jonathan's lovely erect cock. Reaching forward, she slid her hand up and down his hot, straining shaft. Bending forward, she flicked a glance up, encountering his avid gaze.

"Turnabout is fair play. My turn. You're about to be devoured."

Then she took his cock into her mouth, the flavor compelling, and sucked him deep.

* * * *

Ed sat at the bar in the Double Diamond, one eye on the entrance to the lounge, the other on his reflection in the flawlessly polished mirror.

The lighting in this elegant, upscale lounge favored him. Though in full light his face disappointingly showed him the beginnings of crow's feet, this mirror in this light revealed none. In fact, he thought he'd never looked younger, or more handsome.

Of course, when it was time to run for office—and he'd decided he'd start at Senator—he'd likely have a trace of silver painted into his hair at the temples. Yes, that would be striking, and would suggest wisdom and experience to Joe voter without his having to say a word or pay a dollar.

He liked that.

The sounds of the gaming floor were muted here, the music being piped into the lounge jazzy blues. The people who owned this place knew a lot about appearances. The atmosphere was laid back casual with a coating of sophistication.

Movement by the door caught his attention.

Nearly four months had passed since he'd last seen Tabitha. She was, of course, breathtakingly gorgeous. He wouldn't have gone after her otherwise, even considering the money he'd known she would one day inherit. A man had to have standards, after all. She stood at the entrance of the lounge, her hair upswept in a sleek chignon, the red sheath of a gown draping her body, glittering diamond-like sparkles as it caught the light. The column of her neck looked elegant, even queenly. Ed frowned. Once he announced his candidacy, he would have to have an image consultant re-make her so she appeared more young-professional and less society-diva.

She spotted him, and he automatically straightened his posture and sent her his best this-is-your-lucky-day-because-I-want-to-fuck-you-look.

She stepped forward, but she wasn't alone. Two men flanked her. Ed blinked, thinking he was seeing double. Then he realized he was.

The bar tender snapped to attention when Ed raised his hand to signal the man. *Good service here.* Then he turned his attention to Tabitha.

"Baby-face, you look beautiful tonight." He reached for her, intending to give her one of his most seductive kisses.

His hands were blocked by one of the bruisers accompanying her.

"Hello, Ed. You're looking…not your best. Are you unwell?"

He swung his gaze to the mirror, wondering what it was she could see that he hadn't. Then he caught a glimpse of her smirk and it occurred to him she was teasing him.

"That wasn't very kind, Tabitha." She wasn't looking very pleased to see him, and that he couldn't understand. She couldn't *possibly* like being divorced and living all the hell and gone out here. The entire situation painted her a loser. Didn't she realize that?

"It isn't my goal, nor is it my desire to be kind to you, Ed."

The bartender chose that moment to say, "Good evening, Mr. Keller, Mr. Keller, ma'am. What may I get for you?"

"My brother and I will have our usual. The lady would like a glass of Coors."

Ed frowned. "You don't drink beer. It's too pedestrian."

Tabitha laughed. To the man on her right, she said, "See?"

"Sorry I ever doubted you, love," he replied.

"I've always liked beer, Ed. You're the one who's a wine snob."

Ed didn't like the sound of the endearment. It was clearly time for him to establish his position, and his authority. Tabitha was his wife. Well she had been, and would be again before long. He just needed to bring her to her senses.

"Why don't you gentlemen go find something else to do? Tabitha and I would like to have some intimate time together."

"There's a law against that in public places in this state," the man on Tabitha's left said.

"There should be a law about allowing morons out in public, too," the man on the right added.

Tabitha chuckled, but the laugh didn't sound fun. It sounded nasty. Ed tilted his head trying to figure out what had happened to his sweet, empty-headed little blonde.

"Ed Lambert, meet James and Jonathan Keller. They own this casino and are very, *very* close personal friends of mine."

He didn't like the way she stroked her hand down one man's arm while she leaned her back against the other. "You've only been here a month. How the hell can you make a close personal friend in that time, let alone two?" he demanded.

"Kismet," one of the men said. He gave Tabitha a look Ed thought was highly inappropriate for a new acquaintance. Then he pinned him with a gaze that lacked any warmth whatsoever.

"Tabitha doesn't want to spend any intimate time with you. In fact, we asked her to agree to meet with you here tonight so that we could tell you just that, personally."

"And to advise you to leave the lady alone. She's taken."

"Taken? By whom?" This scene wasn't playing out the way he'd envisioned it at all.

It took Ed a moment to realize the only answer he was going to get to his question was three enigmatic stares.

The bartender delivered the drinks, and the man on Tabitha's left distributed them.

"You and I are finished," Tabitha said to him then. "Go home."

He opened his mouth to speak, but the two men seemed to surround Tabitha with their attention.

"So, do you want to have dinner, or what?" asked one Keller.

"We had the 'or what' just before we came down here."

"So we did. Dinner first, then 'or what'," the second Keller said.

"That sounds like a plan," Tabitha agreed in a voice that sounded to Ed like a sex-kitten purr.

Of course he knew better. No woman was less sex-kittenish than Tabitha.

"Mr. Lambert's drinks are on the house," one of the men said to the bartender. Then he flashed a smile that Ed didn't like at all. "It's the least we can do, all things considered."

He watched as his ex-wife, accompanied by those twin smart asses, left the lounge without even a backward glance.

He turned to face the bartender just as the man refilled his glass with the 1991 Cabernet Sauvignon. He'd chosen the vintage because of its full body, flirty undertones, and because it had been the second most expensive selection on the wine list.

His next glass would be the most expensive, and as he sipped it, he'd try to figure out what the hell he was going to do about this unexpected turn of events.

Chapter 12

Phyllis waited until the elevator doors closed on the Kellers and that bimbo who'd accompanied them. She wasn't sure what that little scene she'd just observed was all about, but she was going to find out.

She walked up to the end of the bar and waited for Jorge, the bar tender on shift, to come over.

"Is there a problem with that gentleman?" she asked, nodding toward the man who sat pensively sipping his wine and admiring himself in the mirror.

"I don't think so. One of the Mr. Kellers just gave him carte blanche. Being as it was the bosses talking to him, I didn't listen in, Ms. Demeter. Sorry."

"Don't apologize, Jorge, you were absolutely right not to eavesdrop. I'll guide our special guest to one of the tables and play hostess—since Mr. Keller did, after all, give him carte blanche."

"Yes ma'am. Shall I deliver your usual Perrier with lime?"

"Please."

Phyllis kept her smile in place. She wasn't certain if Jorge truly hadn't overheard any of the confrontation just past or if he was merely covering his very excellent ass. Phyllis smiled. One of the Kellers might have given the guy free booze, but that had been a *confrontation* she'd witnessed.

She took one more moment to consider the black-haired man at the bar. She'd watched him even before James and his brother had arrived. He was a handsome devil, she'd give him that. And he obviously had intimate knowledge of the situation—and that blonde. She had a bad feeling in her belly. Two blondes in a couple of days?

Not likely. The tart in the red dress was probably the same government lackey she'd seen the other day. This meant she'd worked fast and developed a personal relationship with one of the Kellers, probably with Jonathan, as being with the BLM would give her the most in common with him. Actually, that might work to her advantage. But she had to be sure.

Well, whatever was going on, tall dark and handsome over there could likely answer all her questions.

Phyllis hadn't been expecting the Kellers to arrive this afternoon. That was twice now she'd been left looking as if she was completely out of the loop, as if the bosses didn't bother to even communicate with her. Phyllis needed to know what was going on so she could plan her move on James. If she had to schmooze with glamour boy over there, so be it.

Pasting a flirtatious smile on her face, she approached him.

"Good evening. I hope you're finding everything to your satisfaction this evening, Sir."

She watched as he turned and focused on her, noted the way he gave her a very lurid appraisal, then smiled even brighter than when he'd been looking at his own reflection in the mirror. Since his sour expression had been replaced by a smugly male smile, Phyllis knew she would very soon have him by the balls.

"It would appear my satisfaction level is about to increase," he replied smoothly.

"I'm flattered. Perhaps you'd care to join me at a table where we could get to know each other in a slightly more…intimate environment?"

"That would be very nice." He picked up his glass of wine and got to his feet. "Tell me," he leaned close, let his hand trail down her back to settle against her ass. "Is it true what they say about red heads? That they catch fire in bed?"

Phyllis blinked, not sure she'd heard him correctly. Normally if any asshole made such a clumsy pass, she'd either stomp on his instep or kick him in the balls. But for reasons she couldn't articulate, the words he'd uttered and the sensation of his hand on her bottom seemed to get her juices flowing. Maybe, just for the hell of it, she'd play along, give him a tumble.

"Oh, sweetheart, of course it's not true. We don't catch fire in bed. We explode."

Phyllis had the satisfaction of watching glamour-boy's eyes cross. She led him to a corner table and prepared to have some fun while she found out everything he knew.

* * * *

"Tired?"

Tabitha turned to face Jonathan, then walked into his open arms. They were alone in the penthouse, since James had claimed there was paper work he'd been meaning to get to for some time.

"A bit tired. Between the two of you, I seem to be burning more calories of late."

"And we haven't given you much time to even draw breath. I'd apologize for that, but it would be disingenuous of me."

Tabitha reached up and brushed a lock of dark hair off his forehead. "I'm all grown up and everything. And while nothing like this has ever happened to me before, I went into this ménage relationship of ours with my eyes open."

"Did you?"

His voice rumbled deeply and settled low in her belly. There was something so intrinsically sexy about this man and his brother. She knew they were twins, and while their effect on her was identical, they each filled different needs, catered to separate parts of her.

Jonathan's mostly quiet confidence and easy loving soothed and nurtured in a way Tabitha hadn't known she'd needed. In this he contrasted with James, whose sense of fun and drive for excellence made her want to race the wind and spit in the face of fate.

She was likely living in a fool's paradise believing this could last. She'd deal if and when things went for a shit. In the mean time, she fully intended to enjoy every minute she could grab with these two sexy cowboys—as a pair, or one on one.

"Yes, I did." Stretching up, she laid her lips on his. She kept the kiss light, a flirty promise of things to come.

"You're always setting the pace. I wonder if you'd let me take the reins for a change?" She punctuated her question with another kiss. Then she ran her hands down his chest, ending with a slight brush against the erection that tented his pants.

"Darlin', I'm all yours."

As Tabitha led Jonathan into the bedroom it suddenly occurred to her that this was something very rare in her experience: being able to set the pace, the tone, to be the aggressor when it came to sex.

Only she wasn't feeling aggressive. She couldn't contain her smile when he docilely sat in the padded chair where she set him. Taking a few steps away from him, she turned to face him.

And then she began a strip-tease.

She knew she had Jonathan's full attention as she slowly maneuvered the sparkly red dress, removing one arm from a sleeve, exposing a bare shoulder, and then working the other arm out. She'd worn no bra beneath the sheath. Leaving the neckline just above her breasts, she knew she had his full attention.

The look of complete concentration, of growing ardor that showed so clearly on his face and in his lap not only stroked her ego, it fired her furnace.

As she moved coquettishly, as she lowered the dress ever so slowly, the thought crossed that she never could have done this for Ed. Although she'd only had Jonathan and James as lovers for a scant handful of days, her confidence in her feminine power and appeal had already risen dramatically.

Then she dismissed her former husband from her mind, and focused on the handsome hunk before her.

She spun around, and tossed him a coy glance over her shoulder, even as she reached one hand up her back to pull her zipper down.

His gaze followed the slide of the fastener, and Tabitha felt like the most beautiful woman in the world. Holding her dress up with one arm, she twirled back around to face him.

"You're killing me here, darlin'. But it's one hell of a way to go."

"Aren't you the one who told me *I* was in too much of a hurry, just a few short days ago?"

"No, you must have me confused with somebody who looks just like me."

Tabitha laughed. Sex had never been fun before this man and his brother had come into her life.

When Jonathan just smiled and then adjusted his seat in the chair, she dropped her dress to the floor.

"Lord, have mercy."

Now that was a wonderful response to the few scraps she had on under her dress. The thong was as red as the sheath, and since this man had shaved her mons, lay more tightly and, she'd thought when she'd checked herself out in the mirror as she'd dressed earlier, more sexily, against her flesh. She'd donned stockings tonight because she'd had such a great reaction to them the first time, she'd decided they—and the lace garters that held them in place—deserved an encore.

"You like?"

"Oh yes. But darlin', I think you're missing something there on that sexy little body of yours."

"I am?"

"Mmm. My hands."

"Ah, ah, ah," she waggled her finger at him. "There you go rushing things again. Now, I want to do something special for you."

"I have to tell you, Tabby-cat, you're already there."

Oh, he looked ready to pounce. And that was a good thing. "Be that as it may, I want you to place both hands on the arms of that chair you're sitting in. Put them there and leave them there."

"You know, we have a very nice king-sized bed right there behind you. And look, the maid has already come in and turned it down."

"Jonathan? You said you were all mine, remember?"

"Kind of hard to forget, darlin'." He sighed, but did as she asked.

"Now leave them there."

"Yes, ma'am."

Stepping carefully out of the dress that had been pooled around her ankles, she took the three steps necessary to bring her to him. Then she went down on her knees.

He leaned back in the chair to make it easier for her as she worked on unbuttoning, then unzipping his pants. He left his hands on the chair arms, even as he hissed out a breath when she took his hot, hard cock into her hand.

"I love your cock," she whispered, stroking it gently, watching it intently.

"It's pretty damn fond of you, too."

"I seem to recall you mentioning something about tantric sex. Now, let's see. I could just hold your cock, and take the time to examine it in the minutest detail. Study it, visually, from every angle. Maybe I could lean in real close," she put action to words, "and use my olfactory senses to see if there is a change in scent from one part of it to the next."

"Now darlin', I'm all for trying new things. And I know I'm greedy, wanting to feel your wonderful mouth on my cock again, especially since you've already been so generous as to do so twice already...*God*!"

She wrapped her lips around his cock, moving her head down his length, taking him as deep as she could. Slowly, using her tongue to stroke and suction to entice, she moved her head up and down his dick, pleasuring them both. She loved the taste of him, the way he seemed to really love her mouth on him.

"I want my hands in your hair."

A desperate plea, but a plea, not a demand. Even now, impassioned, he was willing to let her lead, let her decide.

She gently pulled her mouth from his cock. Her hand kept pumping him slowly. She smiled at him and felt the effect of the look he gave her settle in her heart.

"Then do it. Do whatever you want."

"Anything?"

"Anything."

How strong he was to be able to lift her off the floor as he got to his feet! He carried her the few feet to the bed. She could feel him shaking, and knew she'd brought him to his limit. But he lowered her gently onto her back.

In the next instant he fairly tore off his clothes. Reaching into the bedside table drawer, he pulled out a condom, slipped it on.

"I'll buy you another," he said just before he ripped the tong from her body.

Jonathan covered her, and she wrapped him in her arms, raising her hips to meet his penis as he entered her. He shivered, and held himself still, and Tabitha rubbed his back.

Then she clenched her inner muscles.

"*Fuck.*"

"Yes, please."

"Vixen," he chuckled, but the humor did nothing to dull his ardor. He began to thrust in her, and Tabitha relished the sensation of his hot invasion, reveled in the sense of fullness. In deep, heavy strokes he took her, and she gave him all she was. She understood the need in him bridged the physical and the emotional, and she enveloped him in warmth and closeness.

"So good," he whispered. "Give me your mouth, Tabitha. Give me everything."

"Jonathan. Yes." She opened to him, his tongue hot and smooth, his lips moist, his mouth voracious. With teeth and tongue and lips she returned his passion with her own. She met each of the thrusts of his hips with demands of her own, pushing her pussy as close as she could, reaching for the climax that teased her, until there was only the joining of their two bodies and the promise of pleasure.

Curled around him, his sweat bathing her, she felt the shivering tremors of completion. So good, so hot, she surrendered to the orgasm, heart pounding, breath heaving, as she came and came in a torrent of ecstasy. Just as her climax ebbed, she felt the pulsing of his cock deep inside her body, received his shout of triumph into her neck, and held him as he gave himself over to his own rapture.

For long moments she held him, the feeling of being smashed into the bed, of having him on her and in her still a particular joy.

"Thank you, for letting me have my head...um sorry." Rolling from on top of her, he kept her close, so they lay on their sides facing each other even as she dissolved in laughter.

"One of those Freudian slips," she choked out.

"There you go." He slid away from her just long enough to deal with the condom. Then he returned to her, and made quick work of skimming the stocking and garters from her body.

"Here, let me get you under the covers." He lifted her easily and in moments was sliding in next to her and pulling the blankets over them both. "I generally sleep on the left side of the bed. Curiously enough, though we haven't shared a bed since we were very small, James prefers the right hand side. So that leaves you, Tabby cat, in the middle, since James will be along shortly."

Tabitha reached up and stroked his face. Then she snuggled in, her head on his shoulder. "In the middle is just where I want to be." She savored the stroke of his hand down her side and the sound of his heart under her ear. And she enjoyed the sensation of drifting off to sleep in his arms.

Chapter 13

Tabitha stood at the entrance to the gaming floor, her eyes roving the dimly lit interior. No sunlight streamed through windows, and no clocks appeared on the wall. The place was far from crowded, but there were patrons about, feeding dollars into the one-armed bandits or shaking dice at the craps table. Croupiers spun roulette wheels and dealers shuffled decks of cards for Black Jack, Caribbean Stud, or her recent personal favorite, Texas Hold 'em.

Her gaze finally found James. He was standing in an area known as the 'pit' talking to one of the women on duty. She stepped fully into the room and felt as if she was stepping into a cavern.

Some slot machines still took coins, so there was the sound of metal on metal; some bells rang, some jingles played as handles were pulled and reels spun in the quest for Lady Luck's favor.

The hum of voices formed a base for all the other sound, and as she passed two men sitting at opposite slot machines at the end of the row, their conversation snagged her attention.

"Hey, Pete, what time is it?"

"Five after nine."

"Oh. Pete? Is that in the a.m., or in the p.m.?"

"That's in the a.m., Bobby."

"Fuck. My wife is gonna kill me. I've been here all night."

Tabitha nearly laughed out loud. One look at 'Bobby' and it wasn't hard to tell he'd been up all night. Shaking her head, she continued on her way toward the pit in the centre of the card and roulette tables.

A zing of thrill tripped her heart the moment James saw her, because his smile was instant and so intimate that the red-haired woman he was speaking with looked to see what had stolen his attention.

Tabitha wondered at the look of enmity that briefly crossed the woman's face. But then James said something to the woman, and headed her way, red-head in tow.

"You ready to go, darlin'?"

"I am. Jonathan said he had to run an errand, and he'd be out front with the truck shortly."

"All right. I'm nearly done here. Tabitha, this is Phyllis Demeter. Phil is Manager here. The best we've ever had." James was looking at Phyllis when he said that, but then switched his gaze to Tabitha just as Phyllis turned to him. "Phyllis, this is Tabitha Lambert."

"How do you do?" Tabitha asked politely, extending her hand. She'd seen and read the expression on Ms. Demeter's face when she'd looked up at James.

The two of them would have to have a conversation in the truck on the way back to the ranch. She didn't think he knew his manager had the serious hots for him.

"A pleasure," Phyllis proved that she could be professional, though she did fail to get rid of all the frost from her eyes.

James put his hand on Tabitha's back, gently stroking in a display of affection that she knew to be completely unconscious.

Of course, that did nothing to ease the chill from the other woman's face.

"Why don't you go on ahead? I'll be out in just a few moments. I just want to run back to my office and grab something."

"All right," Tabitha kept her smile in place as she turned to the other woman. "Nice meeting you."

It was a good thing the daggers being hurled at her back were only imaginary. She'd be dead otherwise.

She slung the strap of her overnight bag over her shoulder, and kept her smile in place as she made her way off the casino floor and then across the lobby. When she stepped out onto the sidewalk and saw Jonathan she heaved a sigh of relief.

"Is he coming, or does he have the proverbial 'one more thing' to do?"

Since Jonathan had turned off the truck and was standing against the front fender, she guessed he really did know his brother well.

"He said he'd only be a moment. He just had to run up to his office for something."

"I've heard that one before," Jonathan said, than saddled over closer to her. "You want to jump in the back of the truck and make out?"

When she looked at him he raised his eyebrows twice and tossed her a wink. Tabitha dissolved into gales of laughter. "And find myself featured on some Internet edition of 'Girls Gone Wild?' I don't think so."

"I don't see anyone with a video camera anywhere," Jonathan pointed out.

Actually there was very little traffic here at the moment, since it was not yet 'check-out' time at the hotel.

"Digital cameras the size of a deck of cards and cell phones with cameras even smaller, trust me, there is *always* a video camera about. Hell, I'm still shivering about our outdoor hi-jinks the other day out in the pastures. Have you downloaded Google Earth lately? Everybody is watching!"

"Well, let's see how fast they are with their shutter fingers." He scooped her into his arms and laid a kiss on her that left her bells rung better than a casino jackpot.

"Nice," she said, taking the time to lick her lips.

"Tabby-cat, you're just asking for it," he warned. Apparently, he was easily stimulated by her tongue. She'd noticed that about

Jonathan. He and his brother were twins, but Jonathan loved having his cock in her mouth, while James preferred to have his in her pussy.

My God, Tabitha you're turning into a sex addict! Your brain has almost completely turned to mush. She'd never spent time thinking like this before in her entire life.

"Now that is a pretty blush."

Tabitha focused as James approached. His smile was pure male arrogance.

"And I bet I know what you were thinking about to blush that way," he finished.

Somehow she was able to control her smile. Tilting her head to one side, she said, "As a matter of fact, I was thinking about how your Ms. Demeter has the hots for you and how she wished me to perdition just now."

"I beg your pardon?"

Now it was James who was blushing. Jonathan laughed so hard that he had to turn around and lean on the truck.

"There is nothing between Phyllis and myself," James said, and he looked so cute, that combination of chagrin and discomfort on his face.

"Oh, I know. And I know there never has been." She lowered her voice, and cursed her fair complexion as she felt her cheeks heat. "When there has been intimacy between a man and a woman, it shows. Men don't usually seem to pick up on that particular vibe, but women always do."

"You're telling me, in your own way, that we've been outted by our casino manager?"

"In a word, yes. I figured you'd want to know that."

"That fact doesn't bother me. Does it bother you?"

"No."

Jonathan had stopped laughing, and had turned back around to face them.

"We're all still feeling our way here, Tabby-cat," he said quietly. "We've been awfully damn intimate in the short time we've known each other. James and I both understand that a part of you is still leery, still getting to know us."

"You both touch me in ways I didn't even know I could be touched. I've experienced more pleasure since meeting you than I even believed myself capable of feeling. But I'm bopping along having great sex and great fun and then all of a sudden it hits me that I really don't know you that well at all."

James stepped forward, and leaned down until she had no choice but to look into his incredible dark blue eyes.

"Darlin', you may not have known us for a long time, but after what we've done with you and you've done with us, you can bet the ranch that you *know* us—better than just about anyone else. Add that to the fact that you're the *only* one who has ever been able to tell us apart, with or without our clothes on..."

He'd let the sentence hang. If he'd planned on making her feel silly, he couldn't have done a better job.

"I'm not trying to embarrass you, Tabitha. I only want to reassure you."

Which proved, she supposed, that they knew her pretty well, too.

"Let's go back to the ranch, darlin'. We have an entire weekend ahead of us," Jonathan said.

Tabitha didn't know why she was feeling this way all of a sudden. But it was time to shake off this strange mood. She was a woman fully grown, and had made the choice, freely, to accept that wanton wager.

Maybe it had been seeing Ed last night, having her past resurrected in her thoughts. She'd made a terrible mistake in judgment, marrying him. When she thought about it she felt stupid and used and raw.

She really did have to put that bastard out of her thoughts. He was the past and these two delicious cowboys were her present. As to whether or not they'd be her future, she supposed only time would tell.

"I hate to ask, but could we go to my office, first? I know it's in the opposite direction, but I'd like to check in, get my messages, and ream out the receptionist."

James chuckled. Taking her face in his hands he lifted it, then just kissed her forehead. "It's not a problem," he assured her.

"Hell, it's not even thirty miles to Carson City, darlin'. Do you want to swing by your house first, too?"

"Yes, please. I need to grab more clothes."

"When we get back to the ranch, we want to try out a few of those toys we bought yesterday."

She'd had a look at all the toys they'd bought the day before first thing this morning. Seeing the vast collection had filled with equal parts arousal and trepidation.

"Now that sounds like a good way to spend a Friday afternoon. So which one of you guys is going to wear that ejaculating butt plug?"

She was met with twin stares of shock.

"Not happening," they both said at the same time.

"Nothing against people who are bi-sexual, darlin', but we are not."

"Oh, I know that. It's just that store had a great selection of strap-ons and, as somebody already said at least once before, turnabout is fair play."

She knew she kept her poker face, but her men weren't having any of it. Jonathan shook his head and reached for the driver's side door of the truck. James motioned for her to precede him around the front of the vehicle to the passenger side.

She was in and buckled up before she realized the brothers were staring at each other.

"Leash and collar," Jonathan said.

"And the paddle," James added.

"And the paddle," Jonathan agreed.

Tabitha kept her smile to herself. It sounded like she was going to have a really good afternoon, indeed.

* * * *

Phyllis stood off to the side, her view out her office window unobstructed, confident she'd been unseen. She waited until the Keller's truck disappeared out of sight.

She'd had her sights set on James Keller, but one look at him and that Tabitha Lambert together earlier and she'd known instantly they were lovers. When she'd come up here from the gaming floor a combination of fury and depression had been swirling within her.

She'd just been standing here, trying to think of what to do next when she'd seen Ms. Lambert and the *other* Keller.

She felt her smile spread, knew it was a nasty one, and didn't care. Oh, she knew just what to do now, and just how she was going to do it, too.

James, she was certain, had no idea that the blonde bimbo was playing him false with his own brother. But she'd bet Jonathan Keller knew damn well he was fucking his brother's lover.

Yes, I'm sure of it. The moment James had come out, Jonathan had stepped away from that slut, giving all appearances of propriety.

Oh, this really was the answer to everything! By the time she was done with them, she would not only have James to herself, she'd have him here, full time. If she managed this very well, she would drive a permanent wedge between him and his cow-poke of a brother, so she would never have to worry about having to spend time in the back of beyond on that Godforsaken ranch.

And once she had James's ring on her finger, she'd get her way and be in control of this casino. Men, she'd long ago discovered, were easily led if you had a firm grasp of their dicks.

She had a dream, not just to own one casino-hotel, but several. She had the brains and the guts to make that dream a reality. All she needed was the cash. And a little help from someone who had a vested interest in seeing things play out her way.

Phyllis stepped out of her office and gave her receptionist a wan smile. "I've a bit of a headache. I'm just going to my suite for some aspirin, lie down for a bit. I'll be back in an hour or so."

"Of course, Ms. Demeter."

Phyllis's suite was in the south tower, the other side of the hotel from the owner's suite. In only a few minutes she was unlocking her door.

A quick glance toward the front closet, the presence of a polished pair of shoes told her she was in luck.

The drapes were still drawn in her bedroom, and the soft sound of snoring emanated from the bed.

Her smile softened slightly at the sight of the sleeping man. He looked kind of adorable, all sleep rumbled, and hugging her pillow close to his chest. Casual sex wasn't her style, but damned if something about him hadn't gotten to her.

Sighing, she walked over and opened the curtains, flooding the room with sunlight. A low groan followed by a big yawn brought her over to the sleeping man.

"Hey, baby. You're dressed. Come on back to bed. I want to get my hands on those luscious tits of yours again."

Phyllis felt her arousal flicker to life. She wasn't certain just why *this* man could stir her. Few ever had. She didn't regret bringing him to her bed, but he was only meant for a romp. He wasn't a keeper. She had another agenda entirely, and so, she knew, did he.

"There's no time for me to come back to bed right now, Ed. You need to get up. I'll order us some coffee. If you still want to get your blonde bimbo of a wife back, I think I may have found a way to make that happen." Actually, she doubted very much if her plan would help him achieve his goal. But she'd pretend she did, and he'd soon believe it, too.

Rather than being hurt when Ed's eyes cleared of passion, she respected his determination and dedication to a chosen goal. That was something she could identify with.

"Order the coffee. Then come and fill me in as I shower."

He'd tossed off the blankets and walked naked to her bathroom. Phyllis did order the coffee, but asked that it be delivered in a half hour. *That ought to be plenty of time.*

Smiling, she began to drop her clothes as she walked toward the sound of running water. Maybe she had enough time for a quick lay, after all.

Chapter 14

Tabitha wanted to hurry.

She had two gorgeous men waiting patiently for her and the prospect of a weekend ahead filled with fun and games. The disquiet that had stolen into her thoughts earlier she banished for the duration. She was in the midst of paying off a bet and having the time of her life. Yes, it had been a wanton wager, and maybe another time, another place, she'd have laughed it off and refused to accept such a proposition.

But she hadn't, and she could see no reason not to continue on for the time being. She had certainly had more fun in the last few days than she'd experienced in the last few years. That alone was worth whatever coin she'd end up paying in the end.

She had no doubt there would be a reckoning. There always was, in her experience. Of course, it would be just like her to fall completely in love with those two randy cowboys when they really only had thoughts of temporary fun and games. Talk of 'playing for keeps' aside, she was certain that's all this experience meant to them and all it really could ever be: fun and games.

Tabitha shook her head and focused on the task at hand. She checked her e-mails, filing away those that required only that, transferring a couple to the appropriate pending case files, and answering one.

Angie, receptionist not-so-extraordinaire, had left for a dentist's appointment before she arrived, so Tabitha took a few minutes to write her a memo, reminding her that it was against department regulations to give out cell phone numbers or addresses of employees to anyone except under warrant. She felt her temper rising as she wrote and thought it likely just as well Angie had been absent. Tabitha had no desire to get the young woman in trouble with her supervisor, but neither could she allow the breach in protocol to go unchecked.

There had been a note from her boss that the lawyers were preparing the contract for the agreement between the Kellers and the BLM. The document would then be couriered to their lawyer. Tabitha figured if the horses were lucky, then sometime in the next six months or so there'd be a new protected and monitored area for them.

She'd been out of the office for just a couple days, and while she still had vacation time coming to her—she'd been fortunate enough to be able to bring that resource with her when she'd transferred here from Washington—she thought it likely she might return to work on Monday. So she sent an e-mail to her boss, advising him of same.

Just as she was closing out her computer she decided to check the phone message centre. There was one, so pen in hand, paper at the ready, Tabitha began to write as the caller spoke.

"Ms. Lambert, this is Deputy Sheriff Derek Hamilton with the Humboldt County Sheriff's Department. It's Friday, nine a.m. We met at the Keller Ranch last Wednesday. I have a matter of some delicacy that I need to discuss with you, in regard to the operations taking place on or around the Keller Ranch. If you could give me a call at your convenience, I'd like to arrange an appointment between us. I'd really rather not discuss this matter over the telephone, and would be grateful if you would keep this call confidential, as this does involve an ongoing police investigation. Here's my number, please call me."

Tabitha had stopped writing, and nearly missed catching the number. When the call clicked off, she left it in memory and put the receiver back on the switch hook.

I wonder what that's all about? Well, she supposed she wouldn't find out until she called. The Deputy hadn't said the matter was urgent, so her response could likely wait until she was officially back at work. There might be something he'd discovered about whatever had him looking around the other day that prompted him to notify the BLM. She had asked him to do so if he'd discovered any activity involving the horses. Tabitha recorded his telephone number on her cell phone, and decided that if she had time on the weekend—and while she was in Humboldt County—she'd give him a call.

That earlier sense of uneasiness threatened to return. Tabitha forced the unpleasant sensation away. It was time to get back to the fun and games.

* * * *

"Where's Mary?"

James smiled as he stepped up to Tabitha and ran his hand down her back. "Visiting her family in Hawthorne for the weekend."

"It's just the three of us in the house, darlin', and no one from the bunkhouse will be knocking on the door. Just you, me, and James." Jonathan said that slowly. James smiled at his brother.

"I see." She took a few steps toward the staircase then turned. A teasing light entered her eyes, and he was glad to see it. During the two plus hour drive from Carson City to home, she'd seemed distracted

"If you think I'm going to cook for you two this whole weekend, you have another think coming."

"Sweetheart, we would never dream of asking you to waste your energy cooking." Jonathan's avowal sounded sincere.

"Good. Just so long as we've got that straight."

"Tabitha."

James took one step toward her, knowing his use of her full name had caught her attention. "Time for you to make another choice. Time to…expand your horizons. Go into the kitchen now, and we'll follow you, make some coffee, chat for a bit, and make gentle love with you. Go up the stairs now," good God just thinking about what he wanted to happen next was getting him hard. "Go up the stairs now, and you'll be choosing another kind of sex entirely. You will be choosing to submit, and we'll get to use probably most of the things I have in this shopping bag. Your choice."

"You're always throwing the ball in my court," she groused, and damned if that wasn't one of the cutest little pouts he'd ever seen.

"Well, then, you'll be pleased to know that once you walk up those stairs—if you walk up those stairs—that will be the last decision you will be required to make for the rest of the day. Oh, and Tabitha? Your safe word is 'wager.'"

For a long moment, she simply stood there, looking at him, and at Jonathan. Had he played his hand too harshly? Her face revealed nothing of her feelings, which only heightened the sense of anticipation that filled him.

She dropped her gaze to the floor. And then she slowly turned around and climbed the stairs.

He cast a glance at his brother. He could tell with that one look that Jonathan was as excited as he was. Jonathan smiled and motioned him up the stairs, letting him know that he was fine if James called the shots.

She stood in the center of the bedroom, waiting. Jonathan relieved him of the bag, opened it and began setting some items out on the bed.

James took a few steps until he was standing right in front of Tabitha.

"Now here are the rules, and there are only three. You speak only when told to, you submit completely, and you obey instantly. Do you understand? And Tabby-cat, there are only two acceptable answers to that question: 'yes, master,' or your safe word. The former leads us to the next step. The latter ends this game here and now."

Her eyes flashed just a brief bit of rebellion—likely in response to his tone to her—and then she lowered her lashes demurely.

"Yes, master."

"Good. Strip. Take each garment off one at a time, fold it, and put it on the chair behind you. Do it now, and do it quickly."

He would never get tired of seeing her luscious body. Her breasts, just the perfect weight to fit in his hand, looked creamy and smooth, her nipples a rosy pink. Her waist was sweetly indented, her hips lushly curved. And the sight of her bare pussy coaxed his cock into getting harder.

When she stood naked before him once more, he resisted the urge to simply take. He wanted them all to get hot before they took her.

"Go to the bed. Retrieve your collar, and take it to Jonathan and *beg* him to put it on you. Oh, and his name is 'master,' too."

James loved the air of defiance, evident in the flounce in her step, as she nonetheless did as she was told. When she was back in front of him again, new collar gleaming in the lights from the bedroom, he flashed a grin that told her that he knew exactly that he'd ticked her off. And he sighed in relief at the little smirk taking hold of the corner of her mouth.

"Now, go and get the ankle cuffs and bring them here to me. And this time, little slave, put a bit more enthusiasm into your plea to have them put on you."

She sent him a sly little look that made him want to laugh out loud, but she brought him the restraints.

"Oh, please master, *please* shackle me."

All right, that was a bit much. The little vixen was very neatly turning this game around so that she was the one in charge. He had the perfect cure for that.

Squatting down, he placed the fur lined cuffs around her ankles. Connected by a chain that was perhaps a foot long, she'd be able to walk if she took very tiny steps. He ran a finger over the top of the cuff, caressing her leg, distracting her.

Then he leaned forward and placed his mouth on her pussy.

Her skin was soft and silky smooth against his mouth, her flavor rich and spicy. He sensed his brother approach.

"Hold still and hush," Jonathan warned her when she tried to tilt her hips, when she gave a little mew of pleasure.

He tasted her essence, lapped her juices as they began to trickle, and knew he aroused her. Hell, he was arousing himself, and the urge to drag her to the floor, to take her hot and fast and deep, was nearly overwhelming. Swirling his tongue over her he stabbed deep, thrusting in and out until he felt her begin to tremble. Her clit was now poking at him, so he sucked it into his mouth, then released it.

Abruptly he stood. Nodding at the glazed look in her eyes, at the way her breathing was rapid and shallow, he licked his lips to entice her even more.

"Jonathan, why don't you get those hand cuffs?"

"In front, or behind?"

"Behind."

He waited until his brother stepped back again. He stepped over to the bed himself and grabbed a single pillow.

Tossing it on the floor before her, he said, "You see how considerate I am of you, slave? I would never ask you to kneel on the hard floor." He reached down, opened his pants. His cock was already hard. He was going to test his own control to the limit.

"I know we've only been together for a few days, but I've noticed a slight inequity here. I've watched that sweet little mouth of yours devouring Jonathan's cock, but I've yet to feel your lips on mine. Why don't you take care of that little oversight right now?"

The sensation of her mouth on his cock was amazing. The little vixen knew what she was doing too, as she moved her head up and down the length of his shaft, as she swirled her tongue along it and sucked maybe just a little too well.

"Stop." He fought his smile when a slight groan told him she didn't particularly want to stop. But she did, and relaxed back, still on her knees.

When she looked up at him a shaft of pure arousal whipped through him. She wore his collar, his chains, and awaited his command in a position of submissiveness. Latent Dom qualities, indeed. He'd have to maintain a tight control on his own impulses. There was an entire realm out there that at this moment appealed to him more than he'd previously believed.

"Get up, Tabitha. It's time you wore something else we bought for you, time we started getting that sweet little ass of yours ready to take cock."

* * * *

What had started out as more fun and games became so arousing Tabitha didn't know how much she could take. Oh, she'd pushed James' 'master' persona, and seen his appreciation of her maneuvering. And then he'd started to eat her and from that moment on she was so hot it amazed her she didn't combust.

She was on the bed, bent over, pillows under her middle, and one pillow under her head. She still wore the chains, still had on the collar.

They weren't speaking to each other as they prepared, but she had no doubt her lovers were communicating.

Sounds told her some but not all of what was happening around her. The drapes had been closed, candles lit. She heard belt buckles clanging and the unmistakable sound of clothing coming off.

Plastic tore, and latex glided.

The bed dipped as James knelt behind her, between her legs. When they'd placed her on the bed they'd spread her as wide as the chain between her ankles would allow.

"Here, now," James whispered. Cold and wet, the creamy substance brushed against her anus, making her shiver. Then his finger, hot, bold, spread the lubricant up and down, turning the lube warm, oily. He added more but the chill was gone, and only the exciting thrill of his stroking remained.

He brought his finger to the circle of her anus and pushed. She couldn't hold back the groan as the twin sensations of burn and arousal kicked her heart into gear. In and out he worked that finger. He'd taken up a circular motion, increased the pressure he used. Tabitha felt the moisture gather between her legs, and whimpered as her arousal climbed.

"More now." More? She didn't know if she could take more without coming. Though he hadn't forbidden it, she wanted to wait, to hang on until she had his cock in her body.

The more he spoke of was a second finger added to the first. The burn was incredible, but she was so horny it actually felt good.

"Look at that pretty ass open for us," Jonathan whispered.

Knowing that he stood so close, that he watched everything his brother did to her added another layer of heat. Her vaginal tunnel began to convulse, looking for something to hang onto and squeeze into orgasm.

He'd been working his fingers in and out of her slowly for more than a few minutes. Then he pulled them out, and she felt him moving.

Something large and round pressed against her anal opening. She felt herself spread to admit it, felt the burning stretch, the growing tightness as it slid deeper inside her than his fingers had been.

Then his latex covered cock stroked her labia, making her lower lips weep and shiver. He slid into her, a slow penetrating invasion.

"Oh, God," the words escaped, uncontrollable. Never had she felt so full, so hot.

"Can you take it?"

"Yes."

She'd forgotten to say 'master' and she still wore the chains. She expected him to say something about the lack. What he said was, "Hold on."

She had nothing to hold on to as he began to pound into her. His cock, hard, hot, stroked in and out of her pussy, caressing her tunnel, her clit, her g-spot. The thrust of his hips moved the butt plug forward in tiny little thrusts, and the sensation was like an extra jolt of electricity to her woman-flesh.

She'd tested his control earlier, but now she knew it had snapped. With each rapid plunge into her he made little sounds, as if his passion had escaped and he was racing to catch up. He bent forward, tenting her, and she felt his fingers brush her clit.

Tabitha screamed with the force of her orgasm, every point inside her vibrating with rapture, more erotic, more exotic than anything she'd ever experienced. Wave after wave battered her until she could barely breathe, barely think. She felt James's cock convulse inside her, heard his shout, and knew he'd come nearly as hard as she had.

Gasping for air, she felt him withdraw, move aside.

Another hand stroked her bottom. "I can't wait. Watching you two has me too triggered. Tell me to stop, darlin', if you can't take more."

"Don't stop." The words came on their own, and she didn't know if she really could take him or not, but in that moment her body craved him with a hunger she barely grasped.

"Don't stop. Fuck me, Jonathan. Please."

Chapter 15

She had to admit, seeing the land like this—with no roads or cars or construction of any kind—made an entirely different impression upon her. Yes, it looked totally different than what she'd grown up with, what she was used to, but beauty dwelled here, too.

The horses were no small part of that beauty. Because she had asked, Jonathan and James had brought her out here again. This sight must be common to them, yet they seemed willing to indulge her every whim.

Outside of bed, as well as in it.

The wager had been that they could make each and every one of her fantasies come true. She'd taken that bet, quite frankly more interested in scratching the sudden fierce itch she'd had for them than anything else. And had discovered, along the way, dreams she'd never fully admitted to having, not even to herself.

Too dangerous.

If her recent divorce had taught her anything, it was that it was too dangerous to place your hopes on anyone other than yourself. And yet these last few days had rekindled that silly dream of finding a man who would cherish her, who would see to her comfort and her needs and just *be* there for her, no matter what. Someone who would think of her and not just of himself. The kicker, of course, is that now she could imagine not just one man in that role, but two.

"That is an awfully serious face you're wearing there, darlin'," Jonathan said from beside her.

The sound of his voice pulled her out of her thoughts, brought her back to the moment. The mid-day sun shone on down on her, a light breeze smelling of rain brushed her skin, and before her a tableau as beautiful as any she could imagine unfolded for her visceral pleasure.

She couldn't share her deepest thoughts. Not yet, and maybe not ever. So she shared what she could, what she'd been thinking as she considered the animals, before her thoughts had turned inward. "Will they make it, do you think? There really are so few of them left. Will there still be herds of feral horses fifty years from now? A hundred? The truly wild horses are *already* extinct. What if these end that way too?"

"They won't. As long as there are people who care, some will survive." Jonathan sounded certain.

"People didn't know, in generations past. They didn't understand the choices they made had impact in the future. But our generation does. We still have much to learn, but at least now we're paying attention," James said.

They turned their horses around and headed back toward the ranch house.

"I've missed this. I used to ride every week when I lived in New York. Then when I took the job in Washington, it turned into something I would do only once in a while."

"I couldn't imagine not riding most days. Couldn't imagine life in the city," Jonathan said quietly. "I go stir crazy if I'm there for more than a couple days at a time."

"I'm not quite as tied to the saddle as Jonathan is. That, actually, is probably the only major difference between us. It's why he's boss here, and I'm boss at the casino. But I couldn't live in the city, full time, either. Two weeks is about my limit."

James rode a horse as comfortably as his brother did. Tabitha realized that they were like two sides of the same coin.

"Well I loved city living, for about a year. But then it just got...wearying. Carson City isn't as frenzied as DC, but this is nicer. I think I like rural living best of all."

"You know, the BLM has an office in Winnemucca, and that's only minutes away," Jonathan said.

"So if you ever thought you might like country life on a more regular basis you do have options."

Tabitha was getting used to the way the brothers could finish each other's sentences. What she couldn't always judge was the meaning behind what they said. So...if she liked it here, she could, what? Move a few miles away and come visit? Or did they mean something else? Her heart pounded in her chest.

Best not go there. I'll just pretend those were rhetorical comments.

When they returned to the saddle barn, one of the men called out. He came over, held Tabitha's horse as she dismounted.

"There's a city dude waiting to talk to Jonathan. I told him you might be awhile, but he said he'd wait. He's planted his ass on the porch. We've been keeping an eye on him. Seems kind of antsy."

"City dude, huh? What's he look like?" Tabitha asked.

All three of the men looked at her with varying degrees of disbelief. She thought it had been a reasonable question. Finally, the hand said, "He looks like a dude from the city. Black hair. Shades. Suit. Oh, and he likes to look at himself...kept darting his eyes at the car mirror when we were talking."

"Ed."

Tabitha bit back her smile, because the brothers Keller had said that one syllable name in the same tone as she had—disgust—and at the same time. They'd sounded like a mini Greek chorus, the three of them.

"Stupid son of a bitch. Doesn't he realize that he just barely missed getting his lights punched out the other night?" James asked.

"I wouldn't say that perception or insight numbered among his faculties, no."

Jonathan nodded. "Depending on what he has to say, I can't promise he gets a pass this time."

"I never asked you to give him one," she said. "Just don't get your ass in trouble."

"You worried about my ass, darlin'?"

Jonathan's smile was sexy as hell. "Well, it is a very nice ass," she told him.

"Since he just asked for me, by name, he likely doesn't want either of you to hear what he has to say," Jonathan said quietly.

"What the hell is he up to?" Tabitha knew that about some things, Ed was completely clueless. But she would have thought even a brain-dead moron like him would have twigged on to the vibes coming from the Kellers the other night.

"Only one way to find out," James said. "Take him into the kitchen through the front of the house, but give us a few before you get there. Tabitha and I will enter through the mudroom at the back."

"That is exactly what I had in mind," Jonathan said. "That way if my fist accidentally slips, I've got witnesses to say I was provoked."

"Trust me," Tabitha said, knowing all the unhappiness she felt about Ed being here came through in her voice, "you will be provoked."

* * * *

Ed had to agree with Phyllis. Anyone who preferred living out here as opposed to Reno, or any other center of civilization, couldn't be all that swift.

Sitting in the chair on the front porch of the ranch house—and he had to admit it *was* a pretty nice house, really—he felt unnerved by all the quiet. His skin actually started to crawl when he caught sight of a fly. *Bugs. God, I hate bugs.* He hoped that damned cowboy would hurry up and come back.

He'd rented the car, and even though he'd told Phyllis that he'd wait until she gave him the green light, he'd decided to just come out here on his own today. She'd wanted to make sure Jonathan was alone before he made his move. She seemed to think James and Tabitha would be here too, but he knew better. Tabitha was as much of a city dweller as he was. Despite the fact that Phyllis claimed they'd all driven away together, Ed was reasonably certain the Kellers would have dropped Tabitha off at her house in Reno.

He knew his ex-wife.

Motion pulled his gaze to the left. Getting to his feet, he waited for the cowboy to approach. He'd forgotten how big the Kellers were. Dressed as he was in rough clothes, cowboy hat pulled low over his head, he looked like one mean hombre.

Ed swallowed convulsively. He just had to remember that *he*, and not Keller, was the urbane one. *He*, and not Keller was the intelligent one. And really, when you looked at things closely, Ed was doing this guy a huge favor.

"I understand you wanted to see me?"

"Yes. I thought perhaps we should have a talk. Just mano-a-mano, if you get my drift."

"I can't imagine what you could possibly have to say that would be of any interest to me, but I can give you a few minutes. Come inside. I need some coffee."

The interior of the place—the elegance of it—impressed Ed. Hardwood floors, expensive furnishings. There was money here, no doubt about it. And at least the cowboy seemed to respect his surroundings if the amount of time he took to take off his boots, put on house shoes and hang his hat neatly were any indication.

"Kitchen's this way."

Ed had a moment to firm up his impression that the Kellers were wealthy. He knew quality furnishings when he saw them. This house absolutely reeked of money. No wonder Phyllis wanted to sink her teeth into the other Keller. Not that he blamed her, really.

It was just a shame he was determined to take Tabitha back to DC once she came to her senses. Otherwise, he could see him and Phyllis making time for each other on a regular basis. That hot little red-head had been right about one thing. She sure as hell had exploded in the sack.

Ed watched while Cowboy Jonathan went about putting a pot of coffee on to brew. He was about at the end of his patience when the man finally turned, leaned against the counter and folded his arms across his chest.

"All right, now what brings you here?"

"A matter of mutual interest."

When the cowboy just lifted one eyebrow and waited, Ed plunged ahead. "Look, yesterday before leaving Reno, you were seen kissing and fondling your brother's girlfriend. I'm assuming that you'd really rather he not find out about that. That kind of a revelation could really fuck a man up, you know? In my estimation, a piece of tail is nice, and all that, but hardly worth the split that would happen between you and what's his name…Jay?"

"James."

"James, right. A piece of ass isn't worth bad blood between you and your brother James."

Ed gave the man a moment to digest the knowledge that he'd been caught. "Now, here's the thing. The problem, as I see it, is *Tabitha*. If it weren't for her, then there'd be no potential falling out between you and your brother, right? And even though she is a trouble maker—believe me I'm certain that cheating on your brother with you was all her idea—I'd kind of like to have her back. And I know that if I could just get her away from your brother, then she'd come to her senses and we could put our marriage back together."

"You mean you're not divorced?"

"Well yes, we are, but that's just a technicality, believe me. She got her panties in a twist the way women sometimes do, and it kind of snowballed from there. I think she just got to the point where she didn't know when or how to quit, that's all."

"So that takes care of you and Tabitha. But what about James? What will he do with no Tabitha to keep him warm at nights?"

It was a relief to Ed that the cowboy was at least bright enough to see the big picture. He gave the man a big smile. "See, that's the beauty of this whole thing. That hot little red-head that manages Aces and Jacks has her eye on him and is getting ready to grab hold of him once I get Tabitha out of the picture. Actually, she was hoping to get to him before I got to you, so she could throw up the fact that you betrayed him—for some reason she wants to start trouble between the two of you. Now, I don't think there's any need to be doing something like that. I'm letting you know about that up front, because us men have to stick together. With Tabatha gone, he'll be missing pussy, and there she'll be. She's hot enough and smart enough that a man wanting to get laid will see her, and grab her."

"And you're telling me all this because…"

"Well, I figured you could pretend to be James and dump Tabitha. Dump her hard, call her a slut or whatever for spreading for the two of you—and let's face it, that's exactly what she is, right? Of course, all women are, come to that. But that's beside the point. If you could do that *today*, then I'll arrive on the scene, kind of timely like, comfort her, and be on my way to connubial bliss in no time at all."

"Sounds like you have everything all figured out."

"Thanks. Of course, it's kind of a shame. I've only had one taste of one of your Nevada wild flowers. That Phyllis is one hot mama, if you know what I mean."

"Oh, I think we all know *exactly* what you mean."

Ed snapped his gaze to the left, the sound of Tabitha's voice sending a chill down his spine.

"Uh…." His ability to think seemed to be impaired.

"You dirty, rotten, self-centered, egotistical son-of-a-bitch! I wouldn't take you back even if you suddenly learned how to use that under-sized cock of yours! I wouldn't take you back if you were the last man on God's green earth!"

He'd never seen Tabitha this angry before, and when she began to stalk toward him he actually took two steps back.

The other Keller—the one who was standing beside her—reached forward and wrapped his arms around her.

"Now, darlin', you don't want to go and spoil Jonathan's fun, do you? After…what is it you call him? Oh, yes, after Ego Ed here went and so thoroughly provoked him, and all? Do you?"

"Provoked him? How the hell did I provoke him? What the hell is going on here, anyway?" Ed knew his voice had risen in pitch and volume. The reason for that was right in front of him. Jonathan Keller was wearing an expression that Ed didn't like one bit.

"You provoked me by insulting my woman, and my brother. By coming here, where you're neither welcome nor wanted and trying to stir up trouble."

"But…but…damn it! That cunt Phyllis got it all *wrong*? She's *your* piece, not your brother's?"

Ed realized as the words left his mouth that those had probably been the absolute worst words he could have used, entirely.

He saw the fist coming. The next thing he knew he was on the floor, his jaw throbbing like hell, stars dancing before his eyes, his nose bleeding.

"Damn pansy went down with one punch."

Ed wasn't certain which Keller said that.

"That's unfortunate. Since he insulted my woman and my brother *too*, I wanted a chance at him."

"Darling, if you hit him after the way Jonathan just decked him, he won't be able to drive away, and we'd be stuck with him here."

"I thought *you* wanted to kick his balls up around his throat, darlin'?"

"Well I did, and I still do. So maybe you gentlemen would like to take out the trash before I reconsider and do just that."

"Damn, our woman's hot when she's pissed, isn't she, brother?"

"She sure as hell is that, brother."

Ed was hauled up to his feet by two pairs of strong hands and marched out the door, but not before one salient fact penetrated his pain-filled brain.

His ex-wife had taken on two lovers who had willingly chosen to share her—which meant he had just blown his plan all to fucking hell.

Chapter 16

The slide of the butt plug being pulled out of her caused a shiver to wrack her spine. The delicious sensation was followed by warmth—James was using a wash cloth on her. He'd also heated the lubricant, so when he touched the silky substance to her anus, it was a welcome caress.

Tabitha should have felt embarrassed, having James perform this deeply personal service while Jonathan looked on. That she didn't, that she felt so at ease with them both astounded her, and gave her something to think about—but later. Much, much later.

Jonathan wrapped his arms around her as soon as she straightened up. Their reflection in the bathroom mirror, his darker tanned flesh pressed against her pale white, turned her on.

He moved one hand up to cup and fondled her right breast, using his fingers to pinch and pull her nipple. This was a new experience. She'd never gazed in a mirror while a lover pleasured her. She liked this. She looked sexy. And watching what she felt being done to her added to her arousal.

"I've waited a long time to slide my cock into your ass, darlin'. Just imagining how hot and tight you're going to be has got me ready to come."

She automatically switched her gaze to meet James's in the mirror. He looked as aroused as Jonathan did. The pleasure on his face as he watched his brother caressing her was intense and real.

"You've got us both ready to come," James said, "with little more than your open, honest responsiveness to us."

"Oh, God." The sex talk had her squeezing her muscles together in an attempt to keep her dampness from sliding down her thighs.

"You are so incredibly sexy, Tabby-cat. I want to watch James fuck you. Come to bed with us."

Jonathan could be commanding when he chose to be. He never let go of her as he followed her into the bedroom. Once James was sitting on the bed, and opened his arms, Jonathan let her go with a propelling little nudge in his brother's direction.

James pulled her into a kiss that was totally hot, his tongue and lips voracious in tasting her. His hands roamed her back, her ass, between her legs until she whimpered her need.

"Hot, baby?" he whispered when he weaned his lips from hers and sampled her neck.

"You know I am. You have me hot all the damn time, the both of you."

Their male chuckles, deep and intimate, settled low in her belly.

James took one of her nipples into his mouth and suckled. Jonathan stroked a hand through her hair, catching the strands in his fingers and pulling her head back.

His mouth took hers with heat and intent, and Tabitha knew she was lost in the erotic haze created by her two lovers.

Hands caressed and aroused. Jonathan pressed his cock against her back, urging her forward until she felt James's hard penis against her belly.

James lifted her and she spread her legs, straddling him so that his latex covered cock nestled against her clit.

"Take me, darlin'. Impale yourself on my cock."

She needed no more encouragement than that. Lifting her hips, she sank onto him, sighing in pleasure as James's cock filled her. She maneuvered gently, slowly, in order to savor the wonder of his movements. Up then down again, the rhythm steady and strong, she pressed her hips forward, rubbing her clit against the hair surrounding the root of his sex.

Jonathan stroked her back, caressed her from her head to her ass, peaking her awareness that they were three, together. James let go one nipple with a wet plop and sucked in the other one. When Jonathan tilted her head back once more, she eagerly opened her mouth for him, her tongue swirling and tasting, his flavor totally rich, uniquely his own. Reaching back, she wrapped her left hand around his latex covered cock, squeezed him, pumping slowly.

Soft and sensuous, long and lush, sexual pleasure wrapped around her, twin ribbons of heart and heat.

James stroked her clit with the back of his hand and her passion ignited.

Need arced through her, arrow-sharp, spiking her blood, speeding her heart. Clawing, climbing, she raced for the finish, grateful when James placed his hands around her hips, adding his power to hers, his hunger to hers. When he stretched out flat on the bed, she followed him forward, followed him down, the new angle empowering her even more.

Tabitha's climax burst with every color of the rainbow, the cascading fullness of spasms overwhelming her system, capturing her so she bowed back, pressing her pussy closer to James, driving his cock even deeper within her. The spasm of his ejaculation into the sheath protecting them both pulsed against her cervix, and her orgasm spiked anew.

It shivered and crackled through her even as hands lifted her off James, moved her to a spot on the bed beside him.

Hot and hard, Jonathan's cock nudged against the tiny rosebud of her anus and pressed forward with a careful, deliberate push.

She felt herself opening, the burning pain building, feeding the final tendrils of her orgasm so that she moaned. James put his fingers against her slit, and as he rolled closer to nuzzle her neck, crooned sounds of approval and encouragement.

"Don't let me hurt you," Jonathan whispered, and she knew he spoke through gritted teeth. The hands holding her fast broke into a sweat.

"Do it. Please. I need to feel your cock in my ass." Where had this lust been hiding all her life? She didn't know, she only knew that she needed to feel him deep inside her ass.

"*Tabitha.*" Jonathan cursed as he sank all the way into her. "Don't move, darlin'. Give yourself a moment to stretch."

She *needed* to move. The pressure was enormous, the pain of his anal possession more than she'd anticipated, but it didn't kill her ardor. Instead, it fed it.

James began a slow, swirling caress of her pussy, brushing her clit. Crying out, Tabitha pushed her hips back, setting the tip of Jonathan's cock just a tiny bit deeper, until it caressed something inside her that sparked an inferno.

"Jonathan. Please...*move!*" The need to move, to stroke, overcame every other impulse, every other urge, even the instinct to protect herself from pain.

"Fuck!" Jonathan was moving in her, his first few thrusts slow and measured, but she could have sworn she heard the tether of his control snap, could have sworn the primitive buried deep inside him, as it was inside every male, finally tore free and seized control.

Jonathan's thrusts became short and sharp, hard and fast, pushing her face into the mattress with ever increasing speed and force. Her legs let go, spreading wider, that unknown barrier of resistance melting under the heat of the orgasm that rose up, volcanic, from the core of her body, that newly discovered point where all erogenous zones now met and converged.

With James's hand on her pussy, Jonathan's cock in her ass, Tabitha screamed as she came, the pleasure so great she thought it might consume her completely.

* * * *

"Have you decided what you're going to do?" Tabitha asked as James took the exit off Interstate 80 toward US 395/Carson City.

"First, I'm going to give her enough rope." James sent a glance her way. Jonathan had opted to stay home today. There were ranch matters demanding his brother's attention, just as there were casino matters he had to see to. Chief of which, he regretted to admit, was firing his manager.

"You're going to let her go?"

"I have to. What she intended to do was unconscionable. But I need to find out what Ed might have told her. The last thing we want is her badmouthing you."

"I'm a big girl, James. I can take care of myself."

James felt his mouth thin in response to that comment. He was quite well aware that Tabitha believed she could take care of herself. He thought so, too. But what the woman didn't seem to understand was that she didn't *have* to take care of herself all the damn time. She wasn't alone. Not anymore.

A part of him could understand why she would have that thick wall of protection around herself. Oh, she joyously shared her body with them. James thought she was pretty damn wonderful and so responsive to the two of them, that her reaction to them alone aroused the hell out of him and Jonathan both.

She could tell them apart. Did she not understand the *significance* of that?

But after having been married to a loser like Ed Lambert, he could understand her emotional reticence. That didn't mean he wasn't getting damn sick of it.

Yesterday, when she'd confessed that she preferred country life, he and Jonathan had both hinted that she could choose country life. She could choose to live that life with them.

But she either couldn't, or wouldn't, see that as an option. Their offer had received no response whatsoever. In fact, she'd acted as if they hadn't said anything at all.

He could feel waves of growing ire blasting him from the passenger seat of the Porsche. He hadn't acknowledged her declaration of independence, and she was getting more pissed about that with every mile.

"Yes, Tabitha, I know you can take care of yourself. But that doesn't mean I can't work a little damage control. We won't have you suffer any bullshit on our behalf."

The silence drew out some, and James was trying to figure out what else he could say to convince her that he meant no damage to her feminine ego when she sighed and leaned back in her seat.

"Okay. Though personally, I doubt very much Ed has contacted her at all. His take would be she gave him bad information, and the fact that he got a black eye is *her* fault. Likely he's already checked out of his hotel and is on his way back to DC. By the time he gets home he'll have it all settled in his head that he'd come here to make amends with me and that *bitch* seduced him and led him astray. "

"Let's hope so. I wanted to beat him into a bloody pulp yesterday. Fucking moron." James could feel his temper rising. Tabitha unfastened her seat belt, leaned over and kissed his cheek. The feel of her leaning in to him, the press of her breasts against his arm and her wonderful woman-scent all worked together to stir his cock. He wondered if he could convince her to stay in town tonight. Either at her house, or the Penthouse. He didn't care which.

"My hero," she cooed in a voice was soft and sultry.

"Smart ass." He laughed, and blessed her sense of humor for relieving his sexual tension.

"Yes. Yes, I am. So I'm guessing then that you do not want me to accompany you up to the office and sit in while you verbally flay and render jobless the lovely Ms. Demeter."

"You guess correctly. Things might get ugly, and yes, I know you can take care of yourself and blah, blah, blah."

"Now who's being a smart ass?"

James smiled when she slugged him in the arm. She pulled her punch, which was good for him, since he was driving her car.

"Seriously, darlin', I'd just as soon not expose you to what could turn into a very uncomfortable meeting. Is there any place you'd like me to drop you? Or maybe you're in the mood to try and relieve our casino of a few dollars."

"Actually, it's such a nice day I thought I'd take in the River Walk, grab a cup of coffee and just sit on a bench. Maybe I'll be lucky and there'll be some kayakers on the river. I really enjoy watching them. And since I can just walk across the street from Aces and Jacks to get there, you don't have to drop me anywhere at all."

He could tell just by the way she spoke that this was something she'd discovered and enjoyed since moving to the city.

"Become a fan of it, have you? Just like a native?"

"I found it my first day here. It's a beautiful view—city landscape, mountains in the background. And trees! I was so glad to see the trees. I'm afraid I had some preconceived notions about Nevada. I had it in my head that the entire state was desert. Seeing those trees just loosened the tension inside me. Of course I had to learn the names of them because they weren't familiar to me. Alders, Freemont Cottonwoods. Leafy and shade bearing, most definitely. But not familiar."

"I guess there's quite a difference in the flora and the fauna between here and DC." He maneuvered her car onto the Moana Lane exit. They'd be at the casino in minutes.

"In some ways it's like a different planet."

"I've noticed some "back east" type trees planted in people's yards, though. So if you had a hankering for a maple or a birch or a poplar, you could order one in and plant it."

"I noticed that too. But that's not fair to the tree, is it? Or the neighbors, for that matter. You'd have to water it so much because of the arid climate. I miss those trees, but I'll just have to wait till the next time I visit Dad to see them."

"So you're planning on staying? I had the impression you'd only moved here to put space between yourself and your ex. Guess I figured that once you got over being pissed with him you'd head back east." He pulled the car into one of the two 'reserved for owner' spots right at the front of the casino. The doorman on duty—a retired Vegas cop name Barney—tipped his hat to let him know he recognized the boss and would watch over the car.

"That is why I moved here. Nevada seemed the farthest away from DC I could get. But," she paused as she got out of the car, stretched, looked around.

"But?" he prompted.

She turned to face him then, and he couldn't help but notice the tinge of pink in her cheeks.

"But the longer I stay, the more I like it."

"Good." It was the most he could say right then. He tried to remember that he'd only known her—had only *had* her—for less than a full week. Short, short time. But sometimes you didn't need a lot of time to know when something was right, when it was meant to be.

As far as he and his brother were concerned, having Tabitha in their lives was both. Now all they had to do was get the lady in question to see things their way.

He wasn't fooling himself. They'd made some strides in that area, but they weren't there yet. And he couldn't help but notice that since that fucking ex of hers had showed up, she'd pulled back, emotionally.

"Good," he said again. Then he kissed her and headed off to fire his manager.

Chapter 17

Since moving to Reno, Tabitha had used this piece of greenery in the middle of the city as a place where she could restore her equilibrium. The Truckee River, though not at all like the rivers she was most used to, had a calming effect on her.

The failure of her marriage had wounded her. At least, that's what she'd always told herself. But now she wondered if what hadn't wounded her more was her own failure in judgment.

How the hell could I have ever thought I loved that bastard? Standing next to James yesterday in the little room off the kitchen, listening to Ed as he trash talked not only her but all of womankind, she'd felt sick to her stomach and ashamed of herself for having been married to the man.

How could she have made such an awful mistake? Were her instincts so far off that she couldn't tell a prince from a prick?

And if so, where the hell did that leave her now? True, she was only having a flaming hot affair with James and Jonathan Keller. She wasn't married to either of them.

But she had fallen in love with both of them. *Shit, I am in love with them both!*

Not good. Not good at all.

"Ms. Lambert?"

Tabitha looked up into a pair of questioning, brown eyes. It took her a moment to recognize the man standing before her. He was out of uniform.

"Oh, Deputy Hamilton. Hello."

"I thought that was you. Nice day, isn't it?"

"It is, yes. I—" she began, but was cut off by the man who seemed a bit ticked.

"I left you a message on Friday. I expected you to call."

"Yes, I'm sorry." Tabitha could feel her face heating, because the Deputy continued to give her a hard look. She kicked the feeling of guilt back. She had nothing to feel guilty about. "I did get your message but I was on a day off, and since you hadn't said the matter was urgent, I had planned to call you tomorrow when I returned to work. Did I misunderstand the situation?"

He must have picked up on her pique, for he gave her a small smile. "No, you didn't. The matter isn't urgent—at least, not at the moment. But when I met you the other day at the Keller ranch, I thought I sensed some vibes there—it seemed to me that one of the brothers was coming on to you—so I thought I should give you a call. A warning, before you got involved with one of them on a personal level. May I?"

He'd pointed to the space of bench beside her. Seeing no reason to refuse him, she moved over to make room for him to sit beside her.

"What I am about to tell you is to be held in the strictest confidence, as it's an ongoing investigation. If you weren't a federal employee, and new to the area, I wouldn't even consider telling you this. But since you are both, and may be called upon to advise in an official capacity, I thought I should give you a warning."

Tabitha experienced a sinking sensation in the pit of her belly. The Deputy's expression lacked any warmth at all now.

"A warning about what?"

"The Kellers have been under investigation by the Humboldt County Sheriff's Department, in conjunction with the DEA and FBI. Certain allegations have been made with regard to activities witnessed and reported in and around the Farenough Ranch over the last couple of years."

"You can't be serious." Tabitha felt everything inside her turn to stone. "You're trying to tell me that the *Kellers* are suspected of illegal activity?"

"Oh, I am very serious. Now, so far, there has been no hard evidence that they have committed any crime. But we feel that it's really just a matter of time before that evidence appears and this case breaks wide open."

"What—" she had to swallow before she could continue. "What crime, exactly, are the Kellers suspected of committing?"

"There have been rumors of a drug ring operating in the County, and that the area serves as part of a pipeline moving illegal aliens up from the California-Mexico border. Additionally, it's been rumored they've been catching wild horses and selling them to buyers overseas—for meat."

Just the thought of one of those beautiful animals being captured and slaughtered made her blood run cold. It was a vile suspicion. Still, a voice inside her insisted on asking questions.

"Then why did you warn the Kellers of that kind of activity if you suspect them of it?"

"So they wouldn't be alarmed if they saw investigators on their land. They think they're better than everyone else, that they're above the law. They also believe they have my confidence."

It seemed to Tabitha that the deputy sounded bitter. As she watched, he seemed to get his emotions back under control.

"Anyway, I wanted you to know. We don't *think* they're dangerous, although you never can tell. Some people are very good at hiding their true selves, so I wouldn't take any chances if I were you."

He got to his feet and scanned the area. "I've got your number, I'll let you know when we get a break in the case."

"Yes. Please call when you do."

For a long moment after the deputy left, Tabitha sat perfectly still, the sordid allegations he'd shared swirling through her mind, causing her heart to pound and her palms to sweat.

One voice inside her head shouted denials. She hadn't known these men long, but she knew them well enough—and they had a solid reputation in the community—that just imagining them guilty of such illegal behavior was ludicrous.

It was the other voice that churned her guts. The one that congratulated her for exercising crappy judgment yet again.

She didn't completely believe the deputy. Perhaps the Kellers were a part of whatever investigation was going on. But she couldn't believe they were criminals. As to her safety, she had no concerns there, despite the fear the deputy had tried to instill in her.

Rubbing her arms, fighting off a sudden chill, she tried to return to the peaceful mood she'd found before Deputy Hamilton had stopped by, but it wouldn't come.

Still, she couldn't deny that an additional thread of unease twined around her previous whisper thin doubts. She would be going back to work tomorrow, getting her life back on track after this mini-vacation and paying up on her wanton wager. So until she had some indication that the deputy's suspicions were true, she'd keep what he'd said to herself and just wait and see.

* * * *

Jonathan hobbled his way from the paddock, his left hand massaging his left thigh which was likely sporting a horseshoe-sized bruise. It had been a while since he'd been thrown and then kicked by a horse.

Son-of-a-bitch, it hurts worse than it had ten years ago.

He imagined that when James and Tabitha got home he'd get a ribbing from the one and maybe some TLC from the other.

As much as he looked forward to the latter, he hoped now that James *would* be able to talk Tabitha into staying in town for a little one-on-one time with him.

Jonathan would have the opportunity to spend some quality private time with their woman soon. Hopefully after he had the chance to rest up and heal a bit. *Note to self: no more getting thrown by bad-tempered stallions. You're not as young as you used to be.*

He had nearly reached the kitchen door when the sound of gravel crunching under tires made him stop and turn his attention to the front of the house.

The black and white Sheriff Department's car came to a stop and the door opened. Jonathan smiled as Sheriff Peter Thompson emerged from the cruiser.

Pete had been a deputy when Jonathan and James were teenaged hellion-wannabes. He'd caught them drinking underage, and after Pete dealt with them, that had been the last transgression either of them had ever committed.

"Hey, Pete. How's it going?"

"Better for me than for you, apparently. What the hell happened?"

Jonathan looked down at himself, noting that the dusty, torn clothing provided a clue if one was astute—and Pete sure as hell was that—that something had indeed happened.

"Just another one of life's lessons. In the battle of ground versus man, ground wins. You here on business? Man, twice in one week I have a sheriff's car on the premises. Neighbors are going to talk."

"Twice in one week, is it? You had a visit from one of my deputies lately?"

Something in the man's tone put Jonathan's senses on alert. "Yeah. Derek dropped by just the other day."

"Is that a fact?"

Nearing sixty, Peter Thompson might look like the quintessential slightly-overweight, graying jovial grandfather. All of which he was. But he also possessed a mind like a steel trap and an instinct for trouble that was damn near legendary in Humboldt County.

Jonathan knew him quite a bit better and respected him a whole lot more than he had when he'd been that teenaged asshole looking for trouble.

"That is a fact. Why don't you come on in. I could make some coffee."

"Coffee sounds good. But how 'bout I make it while you take a minute and clean yourself up. Might have some damage under those filthy clothes needs tending."

"That's more than a possibility. Come on in, then. You know where to find everything. I won't be long."

Jonathan sighed as the heat of the shower hit his abused body. He'd treat himself to a session in the Jacuzzi later. He had a feeling he was going to need it. For the moment, he was clean. A quick look located a few bruises—the biggest of which was that damn hoof print coming to full Technicolor life on his leg. The skin wasn't broken, so he guessed that was something.

Deciding to forgo his usual denim, he pulled on a pair of track pants and a sweat shirt. Groaning, he finally managed to pull a pair of socks on, too.

He checked his watch. Not too bad. Fifteen minutes from start to finish. The smell of fresh coffee enticed him, and he went to satisfy two cravings: caffeine and curiosity.

"Now that looks a mite better."

"And it feels only a mite better, too."

Pete obviously thought that was funny. Jonathan wondered if he was going to have to pat the man on the back to stop him from choking, he laughed so hard.

He hobbled to the counter and poured himself a cup of coffee. Normally he'd go stand with his back to the counter—the same place he'd been when he'd faced that little pecker-head Ed yesterday. But today he opted to sit at the table.

It wasn't like Pete to dance around a topic. That he seemed to do so now puzzled Jonathan.

"You boys have been friends with Derek since you all were kids together, haven't you?"

And because this was Peter Thompson, and there had to be something important behind the question, Jonathan answered him honestly. "We've tried to be, yeah. But Derek always seemed to hold himself back. When we were kids, I never thought much about it. But as we got into our teen years, I just figured he was shy. I even could empathize with that to some extent. I'm not the most outgoing guy. James was always more that way than me. Why do you ask?"

"You never had any run-ins, any set-tos with him? He doesn't have cause to hold a grudge against either of you boys, does he?"

"I can think of nothing any Keller has ever done to cause him to hold a grudge."

Pete picked up his coffee cup, took a slow sip. Jonathan followed suit and tried not to wince. He'd forgotten the Sheriff liked his coffee extra strong.

"Maybe just being a Keller is enough."

"Pete, what's going on?"

"Over the last few months I've been clandestinely investigating my deputy. It started out with a complaint from Rosie Whitman. You may not know who she is—"

Jonathan had meant to hold back his grin but it flashed before he could. Apparently, the sight of it was enough to stop Pete in his tracks—at least long enough to throw him a disapproving stare.

"You hear things," Jonathan said, trying not to laugh. "Seriously. Rotten Rosie is just a name boys learn in these parts."

"That's your story and you're sticking to it. Anyway," Pete puffed out a breath, and Jonathan wasn't certain if the man was annoyed with him or not. "Anyway, Rosie came to me, royally pissed off. It seems that Deputy Hamilton had been cutting himself a deal with a couple of Rosie's girls in exchange for giving them a pass to conduct business in what we might call mobile parlors. Rosie came to me when one of her girls showed up with bruises. It seems Derek was in a particularly bad mood one day."

"That doesn't sound like the Derek Hamilton I grew up with." Jonathan frowned, pushing his cup aside.

"There's more. The State boys busted a ring of electronics thieves involved in identity thefts. One of them claimed to have some information about a deputy sheriff in Humboldt County who would do business in return for any new electronic toy coming down the pipe. Claimed the deputy was a real hard ass, too."

"I'm sorry, Pete. I'm at a complete loss. I don't doubt your information, but all this just doesn't sound like the tow-headed geeky kid we grew up with."

"People change, Jonathan. Now I have to ask you. What did Derek come all the way out here to see you about? I know it wasn't a personal visit because of what you said when I first got here."

"Just to give us a heads-up about the investigation you have going on in this…" Jonathan let his voice trail off as the truth dawned. "You have no investigation going on in this area."

"No sir, I don't. And if I did, I would have called you myself. Your pa and I were damn good buds, back in the day. I got wind of anything happening hereabouts, I'd have called."

"Yeah. Okay." Jonathan ran a hand through his hair. "He said there was suspicious activity, suspected smuggling of drugs, illegals, wild horses. The whole point of his visit was to let us know that if any of us saw him or others on horseback on our land, not to be concerned. Well, son-of-a-*bitch*!" Jonathan finally realized that entire visit had been an elaborate smoke screen. "That bastard is setting us up, isn't he? He's fixing to do something right here on Farenough land."

"That's what I think, too. Now, don't go getting all pissed. I had to alert the Attorney General's office to my suspicions, and the State police got involved when they got that tip from one of their perps. They've assigned a couple of investigators to the case. My understanding is they have Derek under surveillance, and have had for about a week."

"Which is how you knew he'd been here."

"There you go."

"So now what?"

"Now we wait for him to tip his hand. You keep what I've told you to yourself—well yourself and your brother, of course. I don't expect you to keep anything from him. Likely, I'll give you a call in the next few days. The team that's on him seems to think he's becoming a bit antsy. They believe something is about to come down, though they don't know what. When it does, they'll be on top of it. In the mean time, if you or any of your people do see him skulking about, you call. No hero shit. You got that?"

"Yeah. This comes out, it's going to really hurt his parents."

"Yeah. I feel bad about that. But it happens—good upstanding folk have a kid go bad. Sucks big time. But it does happen."

Jonathan walked Pete out to his car—limped was probably a better description. As he watched the sheriff's progress down the long lane, he thought of the too-shy, too-awkward boy he'd known in his youth.

And he recalled being pleasantly surprised when Derek had become a deputy, thinking maybe at last the guy had found his niche.

Just goes to show sometimes you never can tell how people will turn out.

Jonathan hobbled back toward the house. He hadn't heard from James yet, so it seemed likely he and Tabitha would be staying in town.

No need to call his brother to tell him of this latest bit of news. He'd fill him in when he got home. He'd let the two of them just enjoy the time together.

Jonathan grimaced, his battered muscles seeming a little more painful now than they had just a short half hour ago. Just as well they were staying in town. Looked like the only thing on *his* social calendar was a date with a hot tub and the strongest pain killer he could find.

Chapter 18

"I'm so glad you came in today," Phyllis said as she entered his office. She was dressed in what James would call soft clothes. Instead of her usual business suit of skirt, jacket and plain blouse, she had on a more casual sweater and skirt. As he watched her approach, he really looked at her. He'd been aware, in the last couple of weeks at least, that she'd been looking at him not as her boss, but as a man. He'd ignored her, of course, first because it was against the rules as far as he was concerned, to hit on an employee. But added to that, the woman just plain and simply didn't turn him on.

Now as she came closer, he became aware of her demeanor. She seemed as if there was something she wanted to speak about, but didn't know if she should. She was, he realized, trying to affect a shy and demure persona—when he knew her to be anything but.

"I had a few things I needed to take care of, the sooner the better."

"Well I am glad to see you, even though I was hoping to have a bit more time. There's something I feel I must discuss with you…I was hoping I'd have enough time so that I could find the right words." Her lip trembled, and she cast her eyes downward, as if searching for the courage to do something unpleasant.

"Really? I've discovered the best way to tackle difficult topics is to just…spit it out." And that is just what he should do now, James thought. He'd just wait for Phyllis to put her foot in it, just a little. He wasn't a man to play games, but that wasn't what this was about. Until she gave some indication that she did, indeed, plan to act in an unconscionable fashion, he really had no reason to fire her.

"Very well." She seemed to gather herself. "Before you left yesterday, I happened to look out the front...I was just looking outside the way you do sometimes, and I saw—oh dear, this is harder than I thought—I saw you brother and your girlfriend kissing."

James raised one eyebrow. "Kissing is an accepted form of greeting, especially in my family. I would expect Jonathan to kiss Tabitha."

"Well, yes, I suppose. But it was more than that kind of kiss. They appeared very intimate. I...I do believe he caressed her breast." Phyllis took another deep breath. "And this isn't the first time that it's come to my attention that your brother has done something that might be construed as an attack against you."

"It's not?"

"I've heard reports from staff...words he's said, derogatory comments. I've wanted to tell you for the longest time, but I haven't known how. But this latest—this goes beyond the pale. Something needs to be done. James," she stepped forward, reached out her hand as if in angelic supplication. Then, seeming to think better of it, pulled her hand back. Once more she flicked her glance down in what James perceived as an I'm-not-worthy-but-I'll-offer-myself-anyway kind of gesture. "James," she entreated again, apparently somehow having found the strength, "I'm so sorry. But it's clear to everyone that Jonathan is no friend of yours. I know how much it must hurt, hearing this. I wish there was something I could do to help ease your pain, but it's time for you to face the truth. I've heard it said that sometimes, with womb mates, one is born the good twin, the other the evil one. I know you're good, down to your soul. But Jonathan—Jonathan is not."

Because he felt like laughing, James coughed. He got up from his chair and turned his back to her as if overcome by grief. Looking out the window, he could see Tabitha making her way back toward Aces and Jacks. She was walking slowly as if lost in a world of her own.

The need to be with her as soon as possible swamped him. Why was he spending time with this witch when his woman needed him? He didn't know where that certainty had come from, but he could not deny it was there.

He would deal with this now, and deal with it quickly.

"There is something you can do to help." He turned then and faced her. "Have your letter of resignation on my desk within the hour. Security is waiting outside my door and will accompany you from the moment you leave my office until you are off the premises. Pick a hotel, any hotel. We'll pay for your room for the next two weeks.

"You'll be provided with a generous severance, and references. No resignation, no generous severance or anything else for that matter. And I am considering having charges laid."

"I…I don't understand."

"Ed Lambert came out to the ranch yesterday. He left in considerable pain. After telling us the entire plan, of course. Your plan to cause trouble between Jonathan and myself, and then insinuate yourself into my life. Phyllis, that's not ever going to happen."

James was amazed. She made quite the metamorphosis, from concerned loving friend to vengeful bitch in five seconds flat.

"That fucking little prick! I never should have trusted that bastard."

"He expressed similar sentiments about you. You know, I think the two of you may be supremely suited to one another."

"Fuck you. And fuck this place." The smile she took on then gave James shivers. "You may think this was all a scheme, and maybe it was. But I didn't make up that bit about seeing your bimbo and your brother getting it in on together outside. Why, she's probably with him right now giving him the ride of his life. He's such a cowboy it's probably the best lay he'll ever have."

James took one step forward, his fury so sharp he wondered if, for the first time in his life, he would actually strike a woman.

"One more word and you will lose every bit of good will I am extending to you. Letter on my desk in one hour."

"Fine. I'll take your 'good will.'"

When she flung open the door, James caught sight of the two security people—one male, one female—who awaited her. He nodded to them, knowing they'd stay with Phyllis until she was off his property.

James took another look out his window. Beyond, the park shimmered in the midday sun, and people seemed to be out and about, enjoying the day. Glancing down, he didn't see Tabitha. She was likely already waiting at the car.

He would put the unpleasantness of the last few minutes behind him, and see if he could coax the Tabby-cat upstairs. He found, quite suddenly, that he needed to feel her arms around him, and his around her.

* * * *

She should probably have her head examined.

Tabitha let the heat of the shower pummel her, hoping it would banish the stress that had settled into the base of her spine.

James had come out the front door of the casino, his expression so troubled that when he'd asked her to come upstairs, to stay with him, she'd caved.

"I have to go to work tomorrow. That means I'll need my car." It was the only reasonable argument against staying she could come up with. As the minutes had passed, her belief in her lovers—or rather, in her own ability to judge her lovers—wavered. She wanted him. But she wanted distance, too. She wanted to run away and hide, afraid she'd made another blunder.

"It's all right. We have a vehicle garaged here—one that we sometimes loan out to special guests of the casino. Being the boss, I can use it whenever I want."

Warnings and misgivings aside, she did want to spend another night with him. Her only regret was that Jonathan wasn't there, too. What did that say about her, she wondered.

The sound of the glass door opening alerted her just moments before a hot, hard male body pressed against her back. Hands slid around her waist to cup her breasts. Tabitha sighed, and relaxed into his strength, trusting him to hold her.

Trusting him.

Yes, she did trust James and Jonathan both when it came to her body, her safety. The deputy's sly innuendo about these men being dangerous was way off base.

And the rest?

She would tuck that worry away for the morning, and steal this night for herself.

"Feeling better?"

He'd known something was bothering her. But he hadn't pressed her for details. Reaching up behind her, she wrapped her arms around his neck. The action lifted her breasts and James took advantage of the new position, using his fingers to squeeze and pull her nipples.

"Yes, I'm feeling much better."

"Mmm. Let me just make sure." His right hand left her breast and smoothed down her body. Masculine fingers splayed over her shaved mound. In one smooth move they kept on going until he speared up and into her vaginal opening.

"Oh, God, *yes*. Much, much better."

James reached up and adjusted the water. The spray became a fine mist, more steam than shower. His hand came back to her body, bearing a floral scented gel.

"Jasmine," he whispered in her ear, "did you know the flowers are gathered at night? Apparently that's the optimum time to harvest them."

"Are you messing with me?"

"Physically, you bet. But about the harvesting of Jasmine? No. Anyway, in aroma therapy Jasmine is used for relaxation...and arousal."

Tabitha gasped, because he dipped his hand down to her mons again. He began a circular erotic stroking. Her clitoris, eager to play, poked its head up. James caught the little coquette between two fingers.

Tabitha cried out as a gentle orgasm rippled through her body, subtle deep waves that took the strength from her knees. She shivered because James nuzzled her ear, tasting the lobe and shell of it with his tongue.

"I would have thought relaxation and arousal were mutually exclusive," she murmured as she hung in his arms.

His chuckle was deep and sensuous, darkly intriguing, promising untold sinful delights. Then he shifted her slightly, leaning her forward.

"Here, lean against the wall, darlin', with your sweet little ass pointing at me."

She leaned forward but caught sight of the packet he retrieved from the high soap dish. "I think you planned this," she accused without rancor.

"Well," he said as he donned the sheath, "you did profess a liking for water sports. And you'll be delighted to know the penthouse has its own extra large water heater. At this setting, we can stay hot and wet for hours."

She didn't get a chance to comment on that for he laid his hands on her hip and thrust forward, impaling her pussy from behind, driving deep.

"James!" He felt so much larger in her from behind. Needing to feel more, she bent more sharply from the waist.

"Tabitha, you have the most amazing pussy. And it loves my cock. Just sucks it right in, tight and deep."

His words, the rawness of them, thrilled her. She would swear his cock had just grown, wider and longer. His thrusts quickened, the slap-slap-slap sound of flesh hitting flesh echoing off the marble walls of the shower stall.

His balls kept brushing against her labia and she thought she might melt from that sensation alone.

"Come on my cock, Tabitha. I want to feel your pussy shiver down the length of my dick."

She knew she was close, and there was nothing she wanted more than to do just that, to come and come until she had not one ounce of energy left. She tilted her hips a bit more, stretching, reaching.

James fingered her clit and she exploded in orgasm.

"Yes, baby. Just like that."

He thrust into her one more time then held himself deep. She felt the answering spasms of his ejaculation even as the waves of her own climax began to ebb.

His hands slid from gripping her hips to wrapping around her waist. His cock slipped out of her and he pulled her up, flush against his back.

When the water rained down harder, she knew he'd adjusted the shower once more. A slight plop told her he'd just dropped the condom on the shower floor.

"Let me rinse you and dry you. Then I'll give you a back rub."

"If your back rubs are as good as your foot massages, I might make you my slave for life."

"Promises, promises."

Tabitha refused to think about either those words or the tone in which he'd said them. She felt boneless enough that she knew total relaxation was only a heartbeat away.

True to his word he lifted her from the shower. The heated towels felt like heaven as he wrapped her in them. He held her on his lap on the vanity chair, his motions gentle as he patted her dry.

This was a kind of being cared for she'd never experienced, and it was wonderful. Both James and Jonathan seemed to do this sort of thing almost instinctively. Until she'd experienced it, she'd never really known that this was something she'd craved.

"Here, baby, crawl into the bed and lie on your tummy."

Tabitha blinked as James set her on her feet. *Why, I must have dozed off in his arms.*

It took no effort whatsoever to do as he asked. Gasping because the sheets felt chilled against her skin, she scooted over to the center of the bed.

She heard him padding back toward the bathroom. In moments he returned, straddling her so that he faced her back. He kept his weight off her, and she imagined herself melting into the mattress.

"I'll warm the cream before I massage it in."

"As long as it's not jasmine. Another dose of that and I might die in orgasmic delight."

The sound of his laugher washed over her and she smiled in response.

"No, this is called peaches and cream. First I'll cover you. Then I'll eat you."

It was too easy to toss his words back at him. "Promises, promises."

Tabitha drifted on a plane of what could only be Zen-like euphoria. James's hands, coated with the silky, sensuous cream caressed and kneaded, stroked and soothed until Tabitha was positive she was turning into a boneless, carefree mass. Not one drop of tension remained in her body, not one trying thought remained in her head.

When he murmured and urged her onto her back she complied, certain she was but moments from sleep.

Sly hands smoothed lotion over her belly and breasts, and Tabitha recognized the awakening tendrils of arousal. Her breathing changed from edge of sleep deep draughts to the shallow, almost panting breaths of excitement. His fingers skirted the inside of her thighs, whispered light touches across her belly, dipping coyly down to brush her labia, then deeper to tease and tantalize the swollen nubbin of flesh, the epicenter of her desire.

"Now I'm going to eat."

James's mouth, open, hot, wet, covered her pussy, his lips sliding back and forth over her labia, her clit, while his tongue slipped out of his mouth and slipped into her, driving her toward heaven.

He settled down between her open thighs, spreading her legs up and wide, exposing her completely to his oral possession.

Tabitha's arousal grew steadily, a force of nature totally out of her control, reaching, climbing and taking her with it.

He owned her. His mouth and tongue commanded her and she could only feel, only climb. When he murmured into her flesh, the added vibrations shivered out along every nerve ending.

Then he speared two fingers into her, seeking and finding her g-spot, stroking it with slow, steady deliberation.

He held her when the climax bowed her body off the bed, held her as she screamed and came, as wave after wave of unrelenting rapture washed over and through her.

His mouth voracious, his tongue insatiable, he held her fast, forcing the pleasure on her without mercy.

Finally, finally, he brought her down to a gentle throb, an ebbing ecstasy that shimmered, softly, before edging toward shore.

His arms gathered her close, his heat surrounded her. She tried to speak, tried to say…something.

The crooning sound of his voice, a lullaby, soothed her until she felt the long luscious slide into sleep.

Chapter 19

Derek Hamilton got out of his car in front of Ma's Kitchen in Winnemucca. It was early yet, just shy of seven in the morning. He took a moment to lock his car door, and as he did, discreetly directed his gaze down the street.

The light brown Ford Taurus had pulled in against the curb a block back. The car sat, engine turned off. He couldn't risk a really good look—he didn't want them to know they'd been spotted.

Keeping aware of that parked car, Derek strolled in to the restaurant—one he frequented about twice a week. Tipping his hat to an elderly lady sitting alone in one of the booths, he took a seat on the stool at the end of the counter. He looked around the diner, smiling at the ones who happened to look up. There weren't a lot of people out this early, and he recognized every one of them from old Mrs. Wilder having her Monday morning breakfast out, to Joe Canfield, owner of the garage where Derek took his car to be fixed. Those he didn't know by name, he recognized by face, including the two ranch hands in the booth closest to him. They worked on the Keller spread, but lived in town because they both were married.

Turning his head just a fraction, he could see out the front window and the street beyond. He could see that Ford Taurus just sitting there, its occupants still inside.

There were two of them and he would bet that within the next five minutes, the passenger would get out and come in here. That person would be a stranger. He or she might ask directions, or they might order a couple of cups of coffee to go—but not before having a good look at everyone inside the café, including Derek.

When that happened, Derek would know without doubt that he was under surveillance, because everything so far had followed standard operating procedure. He had no idea how long they'd been following him. He'd noticed them for the first time this morning. He was pretty certain if they'd been tailing him before today, he would have noticed.

"Morning, Derek. The usual?"

The usual was the breakfast special. He'd sit and eat it here at the counter, and tip the waitress a dollar. That was his usual Derek-the-geek routine.

Sticking to routine seemed like a very wise choice at the moment. And it would afford him the chance to sit and think.

"Yes please, Miss Jeannie. You know I have to come in here every few days for your Ma's good cooking."

"I surely do, and Ma and I both appreciate not only your business, but your service to the county."

"Why, thank you Miss Jeannie. That's very sweet of you to say."

"I'll go get you that coffee now."

"Thank you kindly."

Jeannie delivered not only a steaming cup of very fresh coffee, but the day's edition of the Humboldt Sun.

Derek opened the paper with no intention of reading it. Looking occupied, he'd be undisturbed. Looking occupied he could keep his eyes on everyone while he tried to figure out why he was being followed, and by whom.

He could report it to the Sheriff and see what kind of reaction he got. No, likely not a good idea. Whoever was in the Taurus, Derek didn't recognize them—which meant if they were law, they weren't from the county level, or even the local State Police.

He didn't think he'd put a step wrong. He'd been careful. None of his lesser "business partners" would have ratted him out, because they stood to lose a hell of a lot if they did.

And if that had happened then that old fart Peter Thompson would have called him in to the office, given him one of those stares over the top of his glasses and asked him point blank what the hell was going on.

"You have got to be shitting me. No way! She's fucking *both* of them?"

"Shh. Keep your voice down. I'm only telling you what Craig saw. And don't go spreading it around, either. Word gets back we'll both lose our jobs."

The voices came from the booth. The words captured Derek's attention and he focused on them.

"Craig saw them? Doing it? The blonde and *both* brothers?"

"Craig damn near rode up on top them. The brothers were naked, and so was she. Looked like they were having some real good fun and games, what with her tied up to that tree and all. We all thought it was odd, the way she came back with them from the city then stayed the night. Couldn't be government business, could it? Remember how we all thought, yeah, one of them is banging her—though we couldn't tell which one? Well the day Old Bill had us all checking parts of the fence line, that's the day I'm talking about."

"And Craig *saw* them?"

"Yeah. He got an eyeful before he slinked off. The bosses were so hot on that bitch, they never even saw Craig. He said that pretty BLM agent is a natural blonde, too."

"Saw her the other day. I sure as hell wouldn't mind giving her a ride."

Derek had picked up his coffee cup. His hand froze mid-way to his mouth.

Son-of-a-bitch! He lowered the cup, fury kindling in his belly and threatening to burn away reason.

"Here you go, Derek. Oh, is there something wrong with the coffee?"

Only his iron will allowed him to set aside his emotions, to focus on Jeannie and give her the patented good-ole-boy smile. "No, it's fine, Jeannie. Everything's great. Thanks."

He thought he'd been clever, planting that gossip with Tabitha Lambert, hoping to use her to discredit the Kellers, when all the time the slut was banging both of them?

It wasn't hard to connect the dots. He'd bet the cunt had run right back to that fucking casino and told the Kellers what he'd said. He could picture it plain as day, too.

The bell over the café door jangled, and Derek felt the hairs on the back of his neck bristle. It took massive effort on his part to keep his manner calm, to eat his food as if that was the only thing on his mind.

"Well, hi there. What can I get you?" Jeannie gave her customary warm greeting to the new arrival, and Derek tilted his head to get a glimpse of the man.

"Do you sell take out coffee?"

"Sure do, mister. What'll you have?"

"Two black, please."

"Coming right up. You new in town, or just visiting?"

"Just visiting."

Derek timed it well, raising his head, looking at the man as any law man would under the circumstances. He met his eyes, and knew he was face to face with a man who had balls. Held his gaze a moment then nodded in a cordial manner.

Then he turned his attention back to his plate as if having dismissed the man from his radar.

Derek paid attention as the undercover cop—no doubt in his gut that's what the man was—paid for his coffee, then headed out the door. He walked down the street, giving a good impression of having not a care in the world, window shopping along the way. Smooth as silk he got back into the passenger side of the brown Taurus.

Looking at the parked car he had a sudden flash of memory and realized he'd caught sight of a similar car yesterday afternoon. Had those bastards followed him over to Elko, or picked him up there? Did they know about his meeting with Bormann?

The man didn't trust the Internet for discussing details, and so a face to face meeting had been called. Derek hated putting himself at risk like that.

Fuck, how much did those bastards know?

Derek couldn't take the chance of bluffing things out. He had a real sour feeling in his gut and that feeling was telling him it was time to come up with an exit plan. He had some cash put by, but he needed more—a hell of a lot more.

With more money, and a head start, he was pretty certain he was smart enough to disappear off the radar of every police agency in the damn country.

He thought again of that fucking blonde slut. An idea began to form. *Oh, now that is just the perfect plan.*

Tabitha Lambert was the Keller boys' private little whore. They were such 'upstanding citizens' he'd bet that if he took her, they'd pay a pretty penny to get her back. And he would give her back.

Eventually.

* * * *

Tabitha awoke as the sun began to light the sky, phantom images chasing her from sleep. How easy it had been in the dark of night to close her mind to doubts and questions, to push everything away and just enjoy the moment, and the man.

But the sun was shining, another Monday had begun and it was time for Tabitha to go back to work.

Time for her to go back to reality.

Turning her head, she gazed for a long moment at the sleeping man beside her. Her throat burned when she thought of what she had to do now, what she *must* do now.

They'd promised to make each and every one of her fantasies come true, and she had to give it to them. They'd done all that and more.

The last few days had been a dream vacation in a wonderful erotic kind of fool's paradise. But the time had come for Tabitha to embrace the truth: it had only ever been that.

She'd fallen in love with both men, but for the life of her she couldn't see how this scenario could ever have a happy ending. Stay with both of them? How the hell would that work?

And then there was the matter of the pending investigation.

Tabitha didn't for one minute fear for her safety while in the company of Jonathan or James Keller. She'd made herself as vulnerable to them as it was possible for a woman to be, and had felt perfectly safe doing so.

That didn't mean she could close her eyes to the possibility that one or both of these men *had* broken the law.

Deputy Hamilton had been certain that it was only a matter of time until charges were laid. He was a man both Kellers seemed to genuinely like and respect. He was an officer of the law.

A part of her refused to believe the Deputy's allegations, and therein lay the problem.

She had believed herself in love with Edward Lambert. He had quite literally swept her off her feet, dazzled her with his attention. She'd married him in a haze of love and lust, only to discover in fairly short order that she had been completely duped not only by him but by her own instincts. He was a miserable excuse for a human being, and she hadn't picked up on the truth of that at all.

Fast forward to the last few days. Here she stood, feeling swept and dazzled and damn well drowning in a haze of lust and love. Again. Yet the objects of her lust and love were about to be arrested on God knew how many charges, which meant once more she'd fucked up.

She couldn't trust her own judgment. Nearly as damning, she just couldn't, she realized, reach beyond the past to grab hold of the present. Because she recognized that at the heart of everything, she couldn't trust that they would ever come to love her in the way she knew she needed to be loved. Her own husband hadn't loved her that way. How could these two men she'd known for so short a time do so?

Slipping from the bed silently, she scooped her clothes from where she'd dropped them the night before.

Soundlessly she crept into the bathroom. She would shower at home. She couldn't take the chance that James would awaken, hear the water running, and join her.

It would be too easy to stay. Too easy to let this affair coast along until she fell so hard, so far, there would be no going back.

And then they would move on, or be in jail, and where would she be?

She picked up her shoes and her purse and crept toward the door. If the gods were with her, she'd be at work before James even woke up.

"You're up early. What are you doing, sneaking out?"

Tabitha froze, closing her eyes. The sleepy voice sounded behind her, words spoken with humor. She heard the blankets rustle, knew he had sat up.

"You *are* sneaking out. What's this all about, Tabitha?"

She turned to face him, every nerve in her body quivering. "It's just time for me to stop playing foolish games and get back to the real world."

"Foolish games. You think that's all this has been? You don't think what you and Jonathan and I have shared is real?"

Something in his tone fueled her temper. "You know what I mean. It *was* a game, a wanton wager that I lost—or won, depending on how you look at it. The terms of the bet were that I was to give you a few days and you'd make each and every one of my fantasies come true.

Well, you and Jonathan did a pretty good job of it. But those few days are up, and I have to get back to my life."

"I see. You're going to walk out, just like that? You were going to sneak out of here without even saying goodbye? You *are* walking out on Jonathan without saying goodbye!"

His anger fueled her own. "You've got nothing to be pissed about, Ace. We played, and now it's time to put the game away."

"So what, thanks for the fuck, now fuck off?"

Had she thought he was angry? James Keller was *furious*. Memories of fights with Ego Ed just before she'd learned the whole truth about him came crashing down around her. She welcomed the cool, condescending façade that descended over and wrapped around her.

"I imagine we'll see each other from time to time, since you're setting up that refuge. Unless, of course, you think seeing each other in a professional capacity will be too difficult for you to handle? If so, I imagine I can get someone else from the Bureau to 'handle' you."

Now James looked thunderous. Rising slowly from the bed, totally naked, he approached her, a male animal stalking his prey. Tabitha nearly bolted. It took every scrap of will and nerve she possessed not to run, not to flinch, to keep her poker face in place.

When he grabbed her face in his hands and brought his mouth down on hers hard she thought she would melt through the floor.

He pulled his lips from hers, and looked at her a long, silent moment.

"It was only a game to you." He said the words softly, and somehow she found his quiet tone more cutting than if he had yelled.

This was harder than she'd bargained for. Even thinking of the embarrassment she felt listening to Ed in the Keller's kitchen, realizing how very wrong she'd been about him, didn't stop this from hurting. She felt as if her heart was ripping in two. Maybe there was something in her that looked for humiliation in her relationships. Maybe she needed her head examined, seriously. Because she hurt, because she felt guilty, she lashed out. "That's all it was to you. A game. That's all sex is to any man."

"This is about your ex, isn't it? Painting Jonathan and me with his colors is kind of bitchy and unfair, don't you think? Kind of childish?"

"And calling me names when you don't get your way isn't?" Before she changed her mind, before he kissed her again and she begged him for forgiveness, she turned, headed for the door.

Hand on the door knob she hesitated. She hadn't planned on warning him. Maybe it wouldn't do any good. Maybe, down the road, it would land her in more trouble than she could even imagine. But she felt as if she owed them *something*. She bowed her head, reaching for reason, and came up empty. Instead, she went with her gut.

"Watch your back. The Sheriff's department is on to you. They don't have anything solid yet, so maybe…maybe you can avoid being arrested. Tell Jonathan—" throat raw, emotions ready to crumble, she had to stop, had to inhale deeply and clamp down on the tears that wanted to flow, "tell Jonathan I said goodbye."

Then she opened the door and walked out.

Chapter 20

He wasn't altogether certain what the hell had just happened.

James stood staring at the closed door, the soft click echoing louder than if she'd slammed the thing.

Slowly, he turned and searched out his clothes. Grabbing up his pants, he pulled them on, choosing to go commando. His shirt came next.

He had a good mind to go over to her house, break down the fucking door, and turn her over his knee.

It was only a game to you.

That's all it was to you. That's all sex is to any man.

Well, hell. He couldn't deny it had started out as a game—of sorts. They'd had very serious intentions about Tabitha Lambert. But they'd never really come clean with her about them, or their feelings. They'd never honestly told her how her loving them both—and James had to believe she'd come to love them both—was their fondest dream come true.

He and Jonathan *had* played games with her. They'd thought they could keep her so sated, so satisfied, that she'd never want to leave them.

Then, too, if you never offered the words, you never had to worry about having them thrown back at you.

James scrubbed both hands over his face as the realization of how badly he and his brother had fucked up began to sink in.

Only one thing to do, and that was go get Jonathan, then storm the lady's ramparts.

Two quick calls had one staff member meet him in the lobby with a cup of coffee, and another with the keys to the garaged car—a 2009 Cadillac XLR platinum.

James appreciated the grace and styling of the two-seater roadster. He enjoyed the comfort of the ride, one of the smoothest he'd ever experienced in a car. And he liked the superior sound system, the On-Star option, and the leather bucket seat that had been made especially for him.

But today what he appreciated most of all was the speed.

The trip from Reno to the Ranch, if one was a law-abiding citizen, took about two and a half hours.

Today he broke the law and halved the time.

Watch your back. The Sheriff's department is on to you. They don't have anything solid yet, so maybe…maybe you can avoid being arrested.

In his anger, then guilt, then need to see Jonathan and tell him what idiots they'd been, he'd forgotten that parting shot.

"Well what the hell did she mean by that? The Sheriff's department is on to us? About *what?*"

The urge to get to his brother flooded him. He couldn't explain this sudden sense of impending danger, but it was one he'd shared with his twin all their lives.

When one of them was in peril, the other always knew. He had that feeling now, stronger than he'd ever felt it. *Danger.*

James floored the accelerator, heading for home.

* * * *

Jonathan didn't even question the inner certainty. He'd experienced it too many times in his life for that. Though movement was difficult, he managed to get his clothes on in near record time. Swearing as he hobbled his way to the kitchen door, he snatched his keys off the counter.

Another beautiful Monday had dawned, the sky so blue it almost looked surreal. Forecasters had promised a sunny, hot day. Jonathan felt a storm in the air and a chill in his soul. His brother was in danger—he pushed away the dozen horrible images his imagination conjured. One thing at a time.

He'd reached the truck and had wrenched open the door when a sound grabbed his attention.

James's silver bullet of a car was barreling down the lane. The car skidded to a stop, spewing dust and dirt sideways as the back end of the vehicle fish-tailed.

James all but exploded out of the car. For long moments they looked at each other, frantic gazes cataloging body parts to ensure the other was indeed safe and sound and whole.

"You're all right."

They'd spoken in unison, and as one slumped against their vehicles.

"Well fuck," Jonathan was the first to recover. He slammed his truck door then took two steps toward James.

"Or maybe not," his brother murmured. He stepped closer, looked Jonathan up and down. "What the hell happened to you?"

"Just a re-affirmation of the cowboy creed," Jonathan said, his face heating slightly.

James barked out his laughter. "Ah, yes. Aint a horse that can't be rode; aint a man that can't be throwed."

"Yeah. It's been a few years, and it seems to hurt a hell of a lot more now that I'm older."

"You didn't have to test the theory. I could have told you it would."

Jonathan nodded toward the house. "The twin alarm pulled me out of bed. Haven't had any coffee yet."

"You slept late."

"Hot tub and a half a bottle of medicinal scotch last night so yeah, I slept late. Where's Tabitha?"

He'd never quite seen that look on his brother's face before. "At work by now, thinking—foolishly—that she has successfully blown us off."

"What the hell did you do?"

"More like what the hell did we do? Let's go get that coffee and I'll fill you in."

Jonathan listened as James replayed his morning. His brother had near perfect recall, and he could clearly see their woman standing there going all ice on him.

"Shit. Guess we should have had a sit-down with her and let her know we really were aiming at building a life together," Jonathan said.

"I can understand her reservations. She's been burned once, badly. And let's face it—a monogamous ménage relationship like we're proposing isn't something you read about in women's magazines...or men's magazines, come to that." James grabbed a couple of mugs off the shelf, filled them with the fresh brew.

"If I hadn't already experienced the three of us naked and having sex like that, I don't know that I could believe it would work." Jonathan reached for the cup his brother offered him. "It does surprise me some that I've never once felt jealous, watching the two of you together. I just felt like this was how, for us, it was meant to be."

"I knew going into this thing that it might be the one time when my hackles might get raised against you. But it never happened to me, either. And I believe the exact same thing. The three of us together is the way it's meant to be."

"Well in that case, we need to get back to Carson City and scoop that woman out of her office. Sit her down and make her understand how we feel about her—that we love her." Jonathan took a sip of his coffee. "She hasn't said the words either, but I know, in my gut, she loves us, too."

"Likely part of the problem, in her mind. She's afraid she'll have to choose between us," James said.

"Well, why wouldn't she come to that conclusion?" Jonathan shook his head, a feeling of self-disgust filling him. "Okay, let me get a little more presentable, and we can go."

"There was just one other thing she said that was strange. And I'm thinking now that maybe it was one of the reasons she kissed us off. But I've been thinking about it and it just doesn't make any damned sense to me at all."

Jonathan had been headed out of the kitchen, but he turned at the door and asked, "What did she say that was strange?"

It took a moment for his brother's words to make sense. And when they did, an awful kind of awareness began to bloom in him.

"Fuck. It wasn't you, and it wasn't me. Damn it, James, it was *Tabitha!*" He quickly recapped his visit from Pete, even as he was heading toward the phone. That feeling of sick dread had returned, stronger than he'd ever felt it.

Just as he reached for the telephone, it rang.

* * * *

If walking away from James and Jonathan had been the right thing to do, why did she feel like hell?

The ache that throbbed in the vicinity of her heart would not go away. Tabitha tried to push thoughts of the virile men aside. She had work to do, a life to live. She had her trusty companion, Sol, for all the lonely, empty nights that stretched out ahead of her.

Damn it.

Fresh before her mind was that damn card game, and the wanton wager she'd accepted. The look on both men's faces when James had said they were playing for keeps had been absolutely serious.

My God, what if they *had* been serious?

A shadow fell over her and she looked up. Deputy Hamilton stood before her. The look on his face sent a shiver down her spine. He was wearing a dark brown jacket. His right hand was in the pocket but he seemed to be pointing that hand at her. Her eyes widened in sudden knowledge and terror.

"That's right. I'm holding my service revolver in my pocket and it's aimed at you. You're going to get up. You're going to slowly walk around your desk until you're right beside me. Then you are going to walk calmly and quietly with me to the elevator. My car is parked on the street, to the left of this building. When we get to it you are going to climb in the passenger side and scoot over to the driver's side, and then you'll drive where I tell you. If you don't co-operate I'm going to kill every single person in this office. Beginning with you."

"I…I don't understand. Why?"

"Well that's two things I know about you. You're a good little actress—and apparently, a good little lay since you've been spreading your legs for both the Keller boys.

"Maybe I'll take the opportunity to find out for myself. I think I like the idea of fucking with their fuck. Now get up."

Tabitha didn't think she could move. One look into Hamilton's eyes convinced her he was deadly serious. Her thoughts froze as she obeyed the man. Once she stepped close to him, he set his hand on her shoulder and squeezed hard.

"No sudden moves, no calling out."

She made her way from her office through the open reception area, very much aware of the open doors of her two colleagues and her boss. The short distance seemed unusually long. Her heart was pounding, her pulse racing. Terror became a lead weight in the pit of her belly and a copper taste in her mouth.

The building that housed the Carson City branch of the BLM also held other federal offices and bureaus. Any other day, Tabitha would have encountered dozens of people. Monday morning, just shy of eleven o'clock, she saw no one.

The sun burned bright in the cerulean blue sky. Once on the sidewalk she stopped and blinked against the strong light.

"Keep moving. My patrol car is right there."

"Won't people talk if I get in and drive? Seeing as I'm a civilian?"

"I don't give a flying fuck. Maybe they'll think you're an undercover cop."

He laughed at his own humor and Tabitha's stomach soured. She knew if she got in that car with this man, there was a better than even chance that she would die.

The door was open and she looked at the yawning maw of the vehicle. Then she looked around and down the street.

Two men were staring right at her. Standing on either side of a brown car, they were focused on her and seemed about ready to head in her direction.

The cold hard barrel of a gun touched the side or her forehead.

The two men saw it and slowly raised their hands.

"Get in."

Tabitha swallowed, then got into the car, scooting over until she was behind the wheel.

The sound of the door slamming behind the deputy sent a shiver down her spine. She held on to the slim bit of hope she had—whoever those two men had been, they understood what was happening. Help would be on the way. She had to believe that.

"Head toward the interstate, toward Winnemucca. Once we're out in the sticks I'll tell you where to go."

Tabitha hoped for slowing traffic, but all the cars before her seemed to part like the Red Sea. It took only a few minutes to get to the 395 ramp.

Hamilton sat with his back to the door, his attention divided between her and the traffic behind them. But his gun was pointed straight at her and she didn't kid herself for one moment into thinking he wasn't aware of every breath she took.

"Yeah, I thought they'd follow."

"Who?"

"Shut up. I'm sick of your innocent act."

"It's no act."

"No, of course not. It's just coincidence that the day after I try to play you by telling you the Kellers are under investigation, I end up with Feds on my ass."

Oh, God. He'd lied to her.

"Those bastard Kellers. They're going to pay."

Tabitha shot her gaze to him, and realized he wasn't even speaking to her. His eyes looked wild, and he was sweating.

His grip on the gun was rock steady.

They drove in silence for nearly an hour, and Tabitha felt so terrified she thought she might throw up. Hamilton seemed to be in a world of his own, but every once in a while he'd look at her, get a sick smile on his face, and wiggle the gun.

"Now, let's see what kind of attention we've been garnering." Reaching forward, he turned on his in-car radio.

Without regard to procedure, he picked up the radio mike and began to speak.

"So who the hell's on my ass, anyway?"

The radio crackled, and then the sound of a deep male voice filled the car. "Deputy Hamilton, this is State Police Detective Joseph Specks. Do you want to tell me what this is all about, Deputy?"

"No, you pretty much know what the hell it's all about, asshole."

"Deputy, the charges you were facing weren't that serious, really. But kidnapping and threatening a federal employee puts those charges in an entirely new category. You're looking at very serious prison time. If you let Ms. Lambert pull the car to the shoulder and get out, we can cut a deal."

"Let me tell you the only deal I'm interested in. I want you to deliver a message for me. I want you to call James and Jonathan Keller of Humboldt County. Tell them I have their whore, and if they want to see her alive again, they can meet us at the old Murchison place. Oh, and if I see a cop, or anyone else except the Kellers, I'm going to kill Ms. Lambert. Did you get all that?"

"Yes, we got it."

Hamilton reached forward and turned off the radio.

"Fucking do-gooder Kellers will come, even if you are nothing more than a piece of ass to them."

"Why are you doing this?"

"Money. And payback. The Kellers have lots of the first and they're going to get a good helping of the second. Take the next exit, go right. We'll be at the Murchison place in about half an hour…which should be about a half an hour before your lovers arrive on the scene."

He gave her an appraisal that made her flesh crawl. Reaching toward her, he put his left hand on her leg and began to slide it upward, toward her crotch.

"Think we can find something to kill the time while we wait of them?"

Chapter 21

James kept one hand braced on the dashboard while the other pressed his cell phone to his ear. Thompson had called them at the Ranch as soon as he'd gotten word from the State Police that Derek had forced Tabitha into his car in Carson City.

He and Jonathan had immediately taken to the road, heading south. They'd been driving for nearly forty minutes. He couldn't explain why they both felt every minute was vital. That sense of deep dread that always before had only come when his twin was in danger churned his guts and liquefied his bowels. He knew without asking Jonathan was experiencing the exact same thing.

If Derek Hamilton laid a hand on their woman he was a dead man.

"The Murchison Place? Yeah, we know the place he means. We're not far from there now."

"No more than twenty minutes," Jonathan said.

"You need to know, Pete. Anything he wants—anything at all, he's got it. We'll pay any price to keep Tabitha safe."

"James, I told your brother, and I'm telling you. No hero shit."

"Yeah, Jonathan told me about your conversation. Thing is, the situation changed the minute he took our woman. He knows it, too. The fact that she *is* ours is why she's in danger right now. If you're right, if his goal is to hurt us or strike back over some imagined wrong, then he's scored a big one. Our only goal is getting Tabitha away from him. Nothing else matters. *Nothing.*"

"Now you listen to me, James Keller. The State boys have Derek in their sights. They're holding back so he won't panic, but they have him. I've just been handed a note. There's a rise about a quarter of a mile from the meeting area. There'll be a tactical team in place about ten minutes after he arrives."

"And we'll be on the scene before that." James closed his cell phone then turned it off.

"She's terrified out of her wits." Jonathan's pronouncement conveyed the same fury and fear burning within James.

"I know."

Time had never moved more slowly. All James could think about was getting to Tabitha. He knew his brother felt the same way.

"We'll make it." Jonathan's words echoed in the truck.

"Yes, we'll make it."

Soon Jonathan was taking a side road, one that dwindled to a dusty track. James shot his brother a smile. "I'd forgotten this back way."

"Remember the time we borrowed dad's Oldsmobile and tried to drive this track?"

"Yeah. I remember that we got stuck because it had actually rained for the first time in more than a month and the ground turned to mud."

"We're nearly there," Jonathan said.

"We used to come out here when we were kids. Remember? What could be more fun for a bunch of teenagers? A deserted house with a swimming pond in back."

"Heard the pond finally dried up a few years ago."

"That's a shame. We saw our first naked female by that pond."

"Miranda Anderson," Jonathan said.

James knew he and his brother had been using empty conversation to keep their emotions from boiling over. The land sloped upwards, a gentle rise similar to the one they'd taken Tabitha over the day they'd shown her the horses for the first time.

He thought of her and her love for those untamed creatures. He thought of her naked and needy, lying between him and Jonathan, loving them both.

And he thought of how she'd been in his arms last night, how hot and giving.

"I'll give my life to keep her safe." The words emerged, whether as some sort of premonition, or just a declaration of his feelings, he didn't know.

When he looked at his brother, Jonathan's expression turned haggard and hard.

"I know."

They fell silent, words unnecessary. Jonathan continued to navigate the truck over the rutted trail, the ride rougher than James remembered. They crested the rise, and there, ahead of them was the hollowed out place where the pond used to be and, beyond it, the deserted house.

"We told Pete twenty minutes. That was closer to fifteen."

"Yeah. If we're lucky we beat that bastard here."

Jonathan brought the truck to a stop, and they both flung open their doors.

The sound of a gunshot followed by a feminine scream exploded from the front of the house.

* * * *

"Pull the car up to within ten feet of that tree there."

Tabitha's nerves were stretched tight. Terror had spread a film of perspiration on her skin. She thought her stomach might be permanently soured.

She brought the car to a stop. Still holding onto scant hope that she could get herself out of this mess, she kept her foot on the brake, but didn't shift the car out of gear.

Hamilton had been sporadically rambling, his conversations with himself sounding like the litany of a petulant child. There'd been no spot on the road where she thought she might have been able to drive erratically and escape. No convenient cliffs to drive toward, jumping out of the car at the last moment. She'd been too terrified, really, to think of any kind of a concrete plan to save herself.

He seemed to be staring at the house before them, as if he was in a little world of his own, as if he'd forgotten her. Boards nailed up where she knew windows should be clued her in that the place was deserted. Now if he would just get out of the car, she'd floor it and be out of there.

Hamilton opened the door. Then he turned and gave her a really nasty smile.

Leveling the gun at her he said, "Put it in park."

Tabitha's heart sank as she obeyed. He reached forward, snagged the keys out of the ignition.

"Now we're getting out, and we're going to have some fun. So slide that little ass of yours on over here."

How far back were the cops that had been following them? She knew that once they were contacted, James and Jonathan would be on their way. How long until they got here? Swallowing convulsively, she began to slide toward Hamilton. She hoped to God this was all over before they arrived. She was filled with equal parts hope and dread at the thought that James and Jonathan might actually show up here.

Derek Hamilton hated her men. If he saw them, he might very well try to kill them.

Her men.

She was nearly out of the car when he yanked her arm hard, pulling her the rest of the way. Stumbling, she fell to the ground.

"Get up."

He stood back a bit, giving her room to move. The moment she was on her feet, he grabbed her and shoved her against the front fender of the car.

"That first time I met you, I thought you were a really nice lady. Thought I wouldn't mind getting to know you a little bit better. But you're no lady, are you?" He reached out and grabbed her right breast and squeezed hard.

Tabitha snapped. Screaming, she lashed out, fighting back mindlessly, frantically. Arms swinging, hands clawing, feet kicking, she went at Derek Hamilton. The gun dropped from his hand as he seemed to focus on fending her off.

A vicious backhand caught the side of her face, and the force of the blow shoved her back against the car.

Her cheek stung, her eyes watered, and she fought off the urge to cry. Derek grabbed her, spinning her around and slamming her hard against the car. She struggled to breathe even as he wrenched her arms behind her back. The sound of clanging metal preceded the sensation of cold steel being snapped around her wrists.

"Bitch. You'll pay for that."

Leaning against the car, she drew in one deep breath, and then another. She squeaked when he hauled her up, over his shoulder. He carried her to the rear of the car. When he opened the trunk, she thought he was going to dump her in it. But he grabbed something out of it, then carried her away from the vehicle.

She fought dizziness when he swung her off his shoulder, turned her around, and laid her belly down on the ground.

She had no idea what he was doing, the sounds both foreign and ominous. Hamilton huffed a breath an instant before she heard a wisp, like the air being sliced by something, followed by a tap, and then a slither.

She felt him kneel beside her, felt his touch on the handcuffs he'd so recently slapped on her. Her arms fell to her sides when the lock released, but her freedom was short lived. Quick as a heartbeat, he pulled her arms over her head, refastened the cuffs.

She froze when he looped rope through the short chain and tied it.

"I heard you like this game."

His words made no sense until he stepped back and pulled her to her feet. Then, as she watched, he grabbed the other end of the rope and began to pull.

Images from an afternoon spent with her lovers flashed through her mind, and in that moment she hated this man with a passion. He was going to take a beautiful memory and make it ugly.

Arms yanked high over her head, the steel of the handcuffs cut into her wrists as some of her weight was taken by them and the rope. Her toes barely reached the ground.

He stood before her, sweating, breathing heavy. The look in his eyes terrified her. He reached forward, tore open her blouse.

"Nice. How accommodating of you."

She'd donned a front-closure bra after her shower that morning. Regretting it now, she felt her face color when Hamilton opened it, when he gazed at her naked breasts.

"You didn't like me touching your tit a minute ago, you're going to hate this."

She cringed, the feel of his hands on her flesh, squeezing, pulling, churned nausea deep in her belly.

"Now."

He stepped back from her, and she saw that he'd retrieved his weapon, had tucked it into the waist of his pants while he'd tied her.

"Maybe I'll fuck you before your boyfriends get here. Maybe I'll just shoot you. Oh, nothing serious. Just an arm. Or a leg. What do you think?"

Oh God, he was going to rape her and kill her. Beyond the fear, beyond the loathing, one regret emerged, larger than any other.

She'd never told her men that she loved them.

His evil smile added to her terror. Then pointing his gun, he fired.

Tabitha screamed. The shot went wide, splitting wood from the tree, sending shards of it flying. One hit the back of her neck, stinging her.

"Hamilton! Stop!"

He turned to face the two men who'd rounded the house and were even now running forward.

Derek aimed his gun toward them.

"No!" Tabitha's world began to dissolve as she watched the two men she loved rushing headlong into danger.

"Stop right there!" Hamilton screamed, then swung the gun wildly toward Tabitha. "I'll kill the whore right now!"

"No!"

James stepped forward, his hands out in a placating gesture. "No, don't hurt her. Please don't hurt her."

Jonathan seemed to be limping. As they drew nearer, they increased the distance between them.

"You don't care about her," Jonathan said, drawing Derek's attention. "It's us you want. Leave her be."

"Stop. Don't come any closer!"

Both men stopped, and Derek swung his gun between the three of them, clearly confused as to who he wanted to shoot first.

"It's Jonathan and me you want," James said. "Let Tabitha go. You can have us instead. We won't fight you. We swear it. You know we're men of our word. Just let the lady go."

"Liars and cheats! That's what you are. It's in the blood. Wilhelm cheated Orville. Liars and cheats."

"What do you want, Derek? Just tell us what you want, and you'll have it. But you have to let Tabitha go."

"You think I believe that? That you'd give me anything for her? She's just a whore."

"She's not," James said darkly. "She's not. And we'll give you anything at all that you want, because we love her."

"So just name it, Derek. Name it and it's yours."

"You need to kill someone? Kill me. Whatever you want. Just let her go." James's words thrilled and terrified her at the same time.

Hamilton shook his head as if trying to make sense of everything. When he looked at her, Tabitha saw the madness in his eyes.

"You'll confess it. In the paper. That your great-grandfather cheated mine, that the land and the wealth was supposed to be mine!"

"We will," Jonathan said, his usual quiet voice sounding strong. "What else? You're going to need money. And you're going to need an escape route, and a hostage. We can get you all that. You know that either James or I would make a better hostage than Tabitha. Isn't that one of the things that you hate most about us? That we're so rich and important? The cops wouldn't dare make a move against you if you held one of us."

Tabitha noted that every time Derek looked at one brother, or her, the other took a tiny step closer. Now, James was within five feet of the deranged deputy.

Tabitha tested the strength of the rope holding her. She lifted her feet right off the ground. Satisfaction zinged through her, the rope held.

"Yeah. Yeah." He took a step closer to Tabitha, waving his gun in her direction. He turned his head toward James and said, "But maybe I'll kill the whore just to make you suffer, first."

"If you do, you'll get nothing." James's voice was hard, angry.

"Fuck you," Derek said, and started to turn toward Tabitha.

Tabitha lifted her legs together and swung them up, fast and hard, connecting with Hamilton's right arm, knocking it and the gun up and away from her.

James launched himself, hitting the man mid section, tackling him into the ground. Jonathan hobbled forward and kicked the gun out of Derek's fingers. Derek tried to fight back, but James brought his fist down hard on the man's face. As Tabitha watched, Hamilton's eyes rolled back and his body went limp.

"Shit, he's more of a wuss than Ego Ed," Jonathan said disgustedly. "You knocked him out with one punch."

"I'm not so certain. He might be playing possum." James hit him again, his second punch resulting in a sickening crack. Blood trickled out from Hamilton's nose.

Jonathan came over to her, his expression so filled with love it nearly broke Tabitha's heart. She felt her body shaking and her vision blurred.

Jonathan pulled something out of his pants pocket—a Swiss Army knife—and reaching up, sliced the rope. He caught her in his arms, hugging her tight. She collapsed against him and disgusted herself completely by bursting into tears.

"Shh. It's all right, darlin'. We have you. Everything's going to be all right. Don't cry. I love you."

"Here," James had retrieved the key to the handcuffs. In seconds he had them unlocked. He rubbed her wrists, then brought them to his lips, kissing each in turn. Jonathan relinquished her, and James gathered her in.

"In case you weren't paying attention, Tabitha, we both love you."

Sirens screamed in the distance, drawing closer. Overhead a helicopter approached, and hovered for a moment over them before moving off slightly to the south and setting down.

She wouldn't let another moment go by. For a dreadful time she'd feared she wouldn't have this chance. "I love you, too," she managed through her tears. "Both of you."

"Then that's all that matters," Jonathan said.

"You're ours," James said then. "And that, as I believe I said once before, is for keeps."

Chapter 22

Tabitha was glad when the last of the cops finally left.

James and Jonathan had wanted to take her to the emergency room at Humboldt General, but she had refused. They'd come to a compromise; her men had taken her home and called their family doctor, who'd arrived at the Ranch nearly as soon as they did.

Doc Jones prescribed ice for the shiner she was developing and aspirin for the pain.

It was only after the doctor had left and she'd put on a clean shirt that they'd allowed the cops to question her. Jonathan and James took turns holding her as she recounted, again and again, the events that had taken place from the moment Hamilton had shown up at her office until he'd been knocked unconscious by James.

The deputy was being held by the State Police, and it seemed likely he would have to undergo an extensive psychiatric evaluation.

Her men had been simply wonderful, coddling her, taking care of her. Slowly, as she'd recounted the ordeal, as she'd relished the feel of their arms around her, her shaking had eased.

As soon as the last cop car left—that of Peter Thompson, who unhappily was off to talk to Derek's parents next—James scooped her up into his arms. Just then the phone rang.

While Jonathan answered it, James simply settled her against his chest. She wound her arms around his neck, but her attention was on Jonathan.

"Hello?" He listened for a moment, then looked at her and his brother with a funny expression on his face. "What did the man look like?" He listened some more, before breaking into a smile. "Really? Do you have any idea where they're going?"

Tabitha switched her gaze from Jonathan to James. For once, it seemed, one twin had no idea what the other was thinking.

"Is that a fact? Well, thanks for calling. Yes, by all means wait until the plane takes off." He hung up the phone, a huge smile on his face.

"That was Williamson."

"Who is Williamson?" Tabitha asked.

"Our chief of security at the casino," James answered. "I had him keeping an eye on Phyllis just in case she decided to start trouble."

Then, of his brother, James asked, "What did he want?"

"Seems our former manager was picked up about two hours ago by—and here I am quoting Williamson exactly—some black-haired pretty-boy with a huge crush on himself. They drove to the airport. Williamson said they bought tickets to Los Angeles."

Tabitha couldn't help it. She giggled. "Oh my goodness. Phyllis and Ed?"

"That barracuda will devour that man," James predicted.

Tabitha noticed that he didn't sound too upset by the idea. "I think they deserve each other," she said.

"I think you're right," James agreed. Then he carried her out of the kitchen.

"Where are you taking me?"

"To bed," Jonathan answered for the both of them.

Only two words, and her body sent moisture to prepare the way for them. Her soul craved them, her heart opened to them. She needed her men more than she needed her next breath.

But her men surprised her when, after stripping themselves and her and placing her in the center of the king-sized bed in her room, they got in on either side of her and did nothing more than snuggle her in.

"Sleep a bit, darlin'," Jonathan whispered.

"Maybe I don't want to sleep. Maybe I want to play."

"Sleep first. Play later," James said. "Let us have this time to feel you, safe and secure here between us."

She didn't think she could sleep, but she was proven wrong.

* * * *

The shadows had lengthened by the time her eyes fluttered open again. Awareness had her looking first left, then right.

Her men were awake, both propped up with an arm, looking at her.

"Hi." She offered them a shy smile, and was greeted with twin loving looks in return. Everything flooded back—her confrontation with James that morning, the arrival of Deputy Hamilton at her office, and the insane hours that followed. The left side of her face still throbbed, though not as badly as it had. The ice she'd held in place while answering all of the cops' questions was likely responsible for that.

Lying there naked between her lovers, she asked the question that had hovered in her thoughts and been pushed aside earlier.

"How did you two ever get there so fast?"

"We knew. We didn't know *what* or *where* until Pete called—and that was shortly after you'd been taken," Jonathan said.

"We have a kind of sense that binds us, always has. So that one of us knows when the other is in danger, or sick. It's like an alarm system," James said quietly. His hand began to stroke her right arm. "It's a common trait between twins, from what we've learned. It went off when I was on my way home and we each thought the other was in trouble. And then Pete called and we realized that the one sending out the psychic-twin S.O.S. was *you*."

"How is that even possible?" Not that she doubted their word. She knew they'd never lie to her. She knew they loved her, too.

My God, they had risked their lives to rescue her. Derek could so easily have shot one or the other of them out by that deserted house. A shiver wracked her at how close she had come to losing them.

"We've figured it all out," Jonathan said, "and it's possible the same way it's possible for you to tell us apart. We know that you're ticked no one else can, but sweetheart, we really *are* perfectly identical in our physical appearance."

"We heard your cry for help because you're out mate," James said simply.

"And you can tell us apart because we're yours," Jonathan finished.

Their expressions were so serious, and yet so filled with love that Tabitha knew in her heart they spoke the truth.

"No games, darlin'. From this day forward, the three of us. We'll make it work, because we *want* it to work." James' tone of voice sounded very matter-of-fact even as he reached beneath the blankets and brushed his hand across her pussy.

"We've never wanted anything more in our entire lives," Jonathan added as he began to caress and stroke her left breast.

"All you have to do is say that's what you want, too. Say yes, darlin'. We both promise that you'll never regret it."

Their hands on her flesh awakened her arousal. Their words, quietly spoken and sincere, soothed her heart.

James was right. They would make it work because they *wanted* to make it work.

How could she deny what was in her heart? How could she turn away from the kind of love that was so deep, so absolute, that they had put her safety and well-being above all else?

Wasn't that the dream most little girls grew up with? Wasn't that the starting point of every happy-ever-after?

How could she say no to that?

"Yes. Yes, to everything. I love you James," she leaned over, kissed him lightly. "I love you, Jonathan," she turned to her left, and kissed him.

As if that was all they'd waited for, they pulled the blankets off and set to work.

Hands and lips and tongues caressed and kissed, cupped and licked. One lover took her lips in a kiss so carnal, Tabitha's flesh quivered, and her sex dripped. The other lover laved and nipped a nipple before sucking it deep into the cavern of his mouth.

Her head moved from side to side as kisses and whispers bound them. Needing to pleasure in turn, she stroked her hands down, giving her fingers free rein to delve through the hair dusting muscular chests, to tantalize and tease male nipples until twin groans of delight joined her own sighs of bliss.

Her hands reached down, discovered hard cocks, and surrounded them, her stroke and grasp firm and fervent.

Jonathan turned her so she was on her knees, directing her head toward James. She needed no further encouragement to take his cock in her mouth, to lavish moist heat and tenderness as the flavor of him filled her, completed her. Hands on her breasts, on her back, encouraged her oral devotion.

Jonathan had gotten off the bed, moved around to the other side. When he stroked her head, she lifted her lips from James's shaft and placed them on his. Their flavor was subtly different, yet equal in the effect it had on her. Stroking James with her hand as she sucked Jonathan, a peace and quiet joy filled her.

They handed her one condom, and then another.

"We both need to be inside you, darlin'. Will you take us both at the same time?"

"Yes…oh yes, please." She needed this special gift, and needed to give it in exchange. She sheathed both her lovers. Scooting over, she made room for Jonathan to lie down in the center of the big bed as James got to his knees and stroked her back.

Jonathan's cock shot straight up, waiting for her. She caressed him once with her hand. And then she mounted him.

His cock filled her pussy completely, the hot head of it hitting deep inside her body. Her sigh of delight came, unbidden, as she rose and sank on him in a languid, liquid rhythm.

Two hands gently drew her down, two stroked her back and urged her forward. She placed her hands on either side of Jonathan's head.

"Give me your mouth, Tabby-cat."

Her lips slid over his, her tongue delving deep to taste and dance with his. A hand on her bottom aroused, a finger stroked over her anus thrilled.

The coolness of the gel sent a shiver through her, and then the newly silky glide of a finger urged her bottom to lift, her thighs to relax and open even more.

She weaned her lips from Jonathan as James knelt on the bed behind her. Her heart pounding, her blood heating, she looked over her shoulder to see her lover stroke his cock as he brought it to her.

That first touch against her, his heat and strength and girth pressing against her rosebud opening awoke a primal need inside her. She raised her hips then sank again on one lover's cock, swirled her bottom and teased the other's.

James leaned into her, pressing hard. She opened ever so slowly, the burning sensation licking the flames of her arousal higher.

"Yes. Oh yes." She shivered from the beauty of having them both at the same time, at becoming one with them simultaneously.

Jonathan teased her nipples, stretching up to capture one between his lips, to nip, to lick, and finally to suck. James's hand caressed down the length of her back, a fine tremor in his fingers tickling and enticing.

She lifted, sank, stretched back, the rhythm exotic, a primal drum beat of need and want and lust.

"Oh, God," James whispered as his cock sank deep inside her.

Never had she felt so full, so hot. Never had she felt so cherished as together, in tandem, her men began to make slow, gentle love to her.

"I love you, Tabitha," James whispered against her neck as he moved within her, his hips gentle in their rocking action. She knew he kept mindful of her, being careful even as he shivered in the complete erotic delight of being buried deep in her ass.

"So tight and hot," he groaned.

"You're tighter for me too, now," Jonathan said, his hips surging up with deliberation. "I'd wondered. Oh, Tabitha, I love you so much."

"I love you both!" She couldn't hold to the steady pace, could no longer contain the need to give back, to give and take in equal measure. Groaning, sighing, she turned up the volume, jacked up the heat.

"Tabby." The strain in James's voice told her how close he was to the edge. The way Jonathan grasped her hips and tried to slow her pace gave her the same message.

They had faced a man with a gun to save her.

They were trying to save her again. She didn't want to be saved this time. She wanted to soar.

"Give it to me. Your heat. Your passion. Give it all to me. Please."

"*Tabitha!*"

"*Oh, God!*"

Masculine control wrenched free, Tabitha rejoiced in their passion, their need. Giving all gave her more. Taking all electrified her senses and shivered her flesh. Harder, faster, she received their thrusts, taking everything they could give, gratefully.

Twin shouts echoed as she felt the cocks within her stiffen, thrust deep, hold fast, and pulse. The heat of their fluids penetrated the latex and set her on fire. Rapture cascaded through her body as waves of the most satisfying orgasm she'd ever known flooded her completely, her clit and g-spot and that tiny place at the base of her spine vibrating together in perfect harmony. Every muscle in her body relaxed, every nerve ending tingled as she came and came and came.

James's weight rested on her back while aftershocks washed through him. Jonathan gasped beneath her as one hand stroked her head, now bowed over him as if, she thought, in reverence of the experience.

Minutes later, sated, cleansed, her men pressed close on either side of her. Each of her hands was held in a bigger, masculine one. The heat of their bodies penetrated her chilled flesh, the beat of their hearts echoed in her own.

"Your generosity blows me away," Jonathan said softly. He kissed her, his lips seeking and soft.

"That wasn't generosity," she returned softly. "It was greed."

"You'll stay," James said in his customary, not-so-latent dominate way. "You'll stay with us. Build a life with us. For keeps."

"Yes. I'll stay."

They lay quietly for a long moment, sleep drawing teasingly near.

"I know there are rules," Jonathan began quietly, "about poker games."

"Poker games?"

Tabitha laughed because she and James had asked that at the same time and in almost exactly the same tone.

"Stay with me here, please," Jonathan said, just a hint of exasperation in his voice. "I know there are rules, but that wanton wager changed my life, and I have been dying to know. I was dealt two sixes. With the flop and the turn, I had a full house, sixes over Aces. Would I have won, do you think?"

"No. I had a pair of tens. That would have given me a full house, tens over Aces. Beat your hand," James said.

Tabitha felt the silence swell, as both men waited for her to reveal her hand, and she remained silent.

"Tabitha?"

There was just enough suspicion in James's voice to make her smile.

"Yes, James?"

"Darlin', what were your hole cards?"

She waited just a heart beat more, savoring the moment. "Pair of Aces."

"You folded on the turn card when you had won!" Jonathan said, propping himself up on her left, looking down at her.

"You have to know four of a kind beats a full house," James said, mimicking his brother's pose, on her right side. "In fact, four of a kind beats everything but a straight flush—and a straight flush was not possible in that hand."

Tabitha smiled, and her smiled grew to a giggle as she looked at first one, and then the other of her loves.

"I may have folded, but I think, in the end, I won the game. I think we all won."

And that, she knew, was the only thing that mattered.

THE END

www.morganashbury.com

ABOUT THE AUTHOR

Morgan has been a writer since she was first able to pick up a pen. In the beginning it was a hobby, a way to create a world of her own, and who could resist the allure of that? Then as she grew and matured, life got in the way, as life often does. She got married and had three children, and worked in the field of accounting, for that was the practical thing to do and the children did need to be fed. And all the time she was being practical, she would squirrel herself away on quiet Sunday afternoons, and write.

Most children are raised knowing the Ten Commandments and the Golden Rule. Morgan's children also learned the Paper Rule: thou shalt not throw out any paper that has thy mother's words upon it.

Believing in tradition, Morgan ensured that her children's children learned this rule, too.

Life threw Morgan a curve when, in 2002, she underwent emergency triple by-pass surgery. Second chances are to be cherished, and with the encouragement and support of her husband, Morgan decided to use hers to do what she'd always dreamed of doing: writing full time. "I can't tell you how much I love what I do. I am truly blessed."

Morgan has always loved writing romance. It is the one genre that can incorporate every other genre within its pulsating heart. Romance showcases all that human kind can aspire to be. And, she admits, she's a sucker for a happy ending.

Morgan's favorite hobbies are reading, cooking, and traveling – though she would rather you didn't mention that last one to her husband. She has too much fun teasing him about having become a "Traveling Fool" of late.

Morgan lives in Southwestern Ontario with a cat that has an attitude, a dog that has no dignity, and her husband of thirty-six years, David.

Siren Publishing, Inc.
www.SirenPublishing.com

Lightning Source Inc.
LaVergne, TN USA
14 August 2009
154917LV00006B/91/P